THE WILDS

BY JULIA TEWELS

For
Anton Diether

"Want to play King of the Mountain, Del?" Jennifer tasked, leaping atop a ledge like a young mountain goat.

Short of breath, Del shook his head and sat heavily on a lichen-spotted boulder. He tried to swallow a handful of trail mix, but could barely get it down. His stomach was a knot, his throat too constricted to accept even water from his canteen. He felt dizzy and nauseous. *Must be altitude sickness*, he thought, ashamed of himself. He couldn't let the others see his condition.

"Yikes, what's that?" Lonny yelped in horror, pointing at something.

Del leaned over and saw a blackened animal skull, half buried in rotted duff.

"Hmmm," Mr. Dugan said, picking it up gingerly. "What have we here?"

Del peered closer, then gasped. For a split second, he had thought the eyehole of the skull had glanced directly at him.

Something papery and black floated to the ground like a grotesque leaf. It was a flap of withered flesh. Most everyone stepped back, repulsed.

"Looks like a bear skull," Gordon said.

"What killed it?" Page asked, intrigued.

"Mother Nature has her ways, son," Mr. Dugan said. "All right now," he called out. "Let's get the train back on the tracks here." He heaved the skull into the bushes.

This world of limitless silences had nothing hospitable; it received the visitor at his own risk, or rather it scarcely even received him, it tolerated his penetration into its vastnesses in a manner that boded no good: it made him aware of the menace of the elemental, a menace not even hostile, but impersonally deadly.

—Thomas Mann, *The Magic Mountain*

One can see only what one observes, and one observes only things which are already in the mind.

—Alphonse Bertillon

Foreword

I grew up wanting to be a writer. From an early age, I loved to read and was a pretty fair storyteller.

In sixth grade I wrote a short story about a Native American family haunted by evil spirits. The narrator was a great chief. Mr. Roy, my teacher, thought it was good enough to read in front of the class. I was not very high up on the food chain of popularity as a quiet, thoughtful kid who was a flop at team sports. But my story held my classmates spellbound. The twist at the end was that the great chief was dead—and speaking from the Next World. When I finished reading and looked up, the room had gone silent, the kids staring at me, eyes agog. One of the popular jocks started to snicker. Then a cascade of applause drowned him out. For a few precious moments I had their attention and respect. And that was enough.

At age fourteen I read an article in *National Geographic* about Sable Island, a desert isle 200 miles east of Halifax, Nova Scotia, Canada. Known as the "Graveyard of the Atlantic," over 350 shipwrecks lie just off its sandy shores, dating back to the sixteenth century. I fell instantly in love with Sable and asked my parents if I could go as long as I found a way to get there. They said sure, never thinking that I would actually pull it off. I wrote the Department of Transport, Canada's version of the Coast Guard, saying that I was a young journalist, and received permission to go. The waters surrounding Sable are too dangerous for ships to land there. I contacted Bill Chester, a friend of the family who regularly flew his twin-engine Piper Apache to Nova Scotia on business, and he loved my pitch. I asked my closest friends, one at a time, if they wanted to go with me. But when their parents heard that there was no airstrip and we would be landing on the beach, they all retorted *Absolutely not!* A camp counselor finally agreed to accompany me. We had an amazing trip. After a few narrow escapes, we flew back home. *National Geographic* published the article I wrote about the trip—my first published piece.

My first novel, *Flashpoint*, told the story of a longshoreman who tries to prevent a supertanker from bringing liquefied natural gas into New York Harbor—the heat-energy equivalent of 36 Hiroshima-sized atomic bombs. In the book's denouement, the supertanker explodes and *poof!*--there goes New York City. I had just moved to Los Angeles and submitted the manuscript to the West Coast representative of a major press. He liked it enough to suggest rewrites. I made them but he still didn't feel the book was ready to submit. So, I made more changes. Back and forth we went more times than I can count. I finally stashed the manuscript in my garage where it is still gathering dust.

My interest in the horror genre was piqued after watching *Rosemary's Baby* and *The Exorcist*. I read and reread both books on which the movies were based.

The late Peter Straub had been my favorite English teacher in high school back in Milwaukee. When I read his novel *Ghost Story*, a bestseller in 1979, it blew my mind. It's still my favorite novel by my former mentor. By this time, I had read and dissected Stephen King's *Carrie*, *The Shining*, and *The Stand*. I dug the dark realms of the psyche in Rimbaud and Baudelaire's poetry. Ditto in Lucian Freud and Egon Schiele's twisty paintings. Not to mention Lou Reed's transgressive lyrics in songs like "Heroin" and "Walk on the Wild Side,"

What I liked most about *Ghost Story* was Straub's masterly use of psychological horror. All the main characters are forced to face their darkest secrets and reckon with them. Setting them either on the path of self-understanding or on the path of destruction. Straub's central theme is that you have to face up to your past to make it through the present and succeed in life beyond it.

My second novel, *The Stalker*, was published in 1984 by Zebra Books as a mass-market paperback and sold briskly. It is a psychological ghost story that takes place in a haunted seed factory based on my family's former seed-processing plant in Milwaukee. It is available in a new edition from Crossroad Press.

In formulating my ideas of what I wanted to convey in *The Wilds* (first published by Dell Books as a mass-market paperback in 1989), I read and reread Henry James' novella *The Turn of the Screw*. I loved its blurred boundary between the psychological and the supernatural, now known as "Jamesian Duality." The reader is unsure whether there really are ghosts—or if they are just constructs in the deranged mind of the protagonist.

You'll have to read further to see how that duality plays out in *The Wilds*.

My inspiration for this book came collectively from William Golding's *Lord of the Flies*, James Dickey's *Deliverance*, and Stephen King's short story "The Body," (better known as the film adaptation *Stand by Me*).

David Niall Wilson of Crossroad Press is a great guy, and I thank him and his staff for loving The Wilds and bringing it back to life in this new edition.

Julia Claire Teweles

1

Gordon

Gordon Hollos turned off the interstate and started up a steep, mean road into the Sierra Nevada. His hands tightened on the wheel, knuckles cracking. The car, the road, the mountains—everything felt wrong.

It was nearly twilight when he turned onto a dirt track, crossed an alpine meadow, and parked at the gate to the abandoned mining camp. A dilapidated signpost, mounted on a pair of old railroad ties, read WOLF GULCH MINING CO. The gold rush-era mine had gone bankrupt during the Depression, giving way to the summer camp that now bore its name.

Gordon checked his watch. The new camp director wasn't expecting him for another half hour. Tomorrow was opening day; these were the last few moments he would have to himself for the rest of the summer.

He locked the car, jumped a fence, and followed a footpath that mounted the crest of a bare, windswept ridge. Sierra grass grew thick and high around a collection of silver-gray wooden sheds. This part of Wolf Gulch was not in use and had probably not changed much since the mine had opened. Only the caretaker's cabin sported a new coat of paint and a strand of telephone wire. Ted Lisecki, an amicable old geezer, lived in the shack winter and summer.

"Hey, Ted," Gordon shouted. "It's me, Gordon Hollos. I'm back."

No one answered. The cabin door was bolted. *Ted must be down in camp*, Gordon decided.

As he moved around the cabin, a large dog—a Doberman—suddenly blocked his way. It lunged to the end of its tether, bristling and barking in a territorial frenzy. The dog's eyes were as shiny and fathomless as black marbles, almost primordial.

"Get lost," Gordon hissed, angry at having been frightened.

He sidestepped the animal and walked to the end of the path, where a promontory overlooked Wolf Gulch's brood of weather-beaten cabins.

Jesus Christ, I'm really back—what am I doing *back?*

His stomach clutched and he felt a panicky rush, as if he were hanging over the crest of some nightmare rollercoaster mountain, about to make the plunge.

No, no, this is all wrong—I can't be here.

Below, he could see two counselors in the cabin clearing, airing out the tents for the upcoming Wolf Gulch Ordeal, the first overnight hike. Gordon knew that the Ordeal was an annual tradition intended to test the campers' mettle and get them into shape for longer treks. On this hike, the counselors would take a coed group up into The Wilds, a national forest preserve in the nearby mountains.

The Wilds.

Gordon's eyes rose almost against his will to the jagged hulk of the Sierra Nevada.

In the last rays of sundown, he picked out several familiar summits, snow-dusted even in June. The granite crags, roseate and fiercely beautiful, appeared deceptively close. Every rift and headwall, even the stunted Jeffrey pines, struggling for purchase, jutted out with preternatural clarity. A patch of glare-ice winked at him in ominous greeting from a razor peak. Gordon felt his skin crawl.

In The Wilds he sensed that man was at the mercy of tremendous forces poised just beyond the reach of his senses. Meandering trails crisscrossed and forked into innumerable phantom tracks to deceive him. *Could an entire wilderness be haunted?* Gordon wondered. The Wilds was the most desolate high country left in California: a fourteen-thousand-foot barrier rim that sealed off the world; an unrelenting mountainscape where peak followed peak in endless succession. This was savage, brutal country. Pity the unprepared camper who lost his way and ran short of supplies.

Like the Donner Party, Gordon thought, and massaged the throbbing pressure point between his eyes.

In 1846, eighty-seven California-bound men, women, and children had attempted to cross the Sierras too late in the season. Their wagon train was snowbound over the winter at seven thousand feet. In desperation, the pioneers were forced to eat twigs, mice, their shoes. Finally they consumed the flesh of those who had already perished, the bodies preserved by the snow. A few scouts were sent ahead to the Sacramento Valley for help. When the relief party arrived, weeks later, less than half of the Donner Party had survived, subsisting in sooty shelters buried deep under the drifts. Human bones—many from children—littered the snow. The authorities questioned whether those who perished had died from exposure or been killed for their flesh.

Gordon stared at the mountains until white spots danced before his eyes.

Nothing had changed in a year. Nothing.

He felt one of his demon headaches coming on. Freight train headaches, he had called them as a boy, the pressure mounting like steam trapped inside his skull whenever he felt anxious.

It had taken Gordon all year to recover from the death of a camper on a hike in The Wilds at the end of last summer. His hands hardly trembled anymore, and he rarely had to resort to his Valium. The nightmare of finding Cal Wolcroft crumpled on the rocks had ceased invading his sleep. Now sleep was his only refuge.

The camp director had been leading the hikers when he suddenly realized that Wolcroft, the youngest camper, had disappeared. The boy could have lost his way, fallen, broken a leg. Alarmed, the director had sent Gordon back downhill to find him. After a long search he located Wolcroft curled up on a boulder-strewn ledge, his arms wrapped protectively around his belly. A rill of bloody saliva streaked the boy's jawline.

With trembling hands, Gordon turned him over on his back. Cal seemed unusually heavy. *Dead weight*, Gordon thought with

a shiver. *Don't they say a dead body weighs more than a living one?*
He pried away Cal's small pale arms, still crisscrossed over
his stomach. Intestines, gray and steaming, spilled out of Cal's
jacket. The mauled abdomen was riddled with teeth marks.

My God! Only a wild animal could have done this.

Gordon felt an involuntary squeeze in his belly. Fighting
back nausea, he fled blindly down the mountainside, unable to
accept what he had seen. Finally, out of breath, he slowed and
turned back uphill. He couldn't leave Cal's body.

Gordon forced himself to think. What kind of animal had
attacked Cal? A wolf? There had been no wolves in the Sierras
since the turn of the century. The teeth marks were too small
for a mountain lion. A bear would have stayed to protect its kill.

Those could not have been human teeth marks.

A chilly gust of wind made Gordon shudder, startling him
out of his thoughts. He looked up and suddenly remembered
the time. The new camp director, Jerry Dugan, was expecting
him. Dugan's predecessor had resigned after Wolcroft's death.
Wolf Gulch's owners had decided it was just a freak incident,
a one-time calamity. And so there had been no cancellation of
this year's Ordeal. It was, after all, an annual tradition.

Gordon trudged back toward his car. Returning to Wolf
Gulch was the hardest thing he had ever done. But everything
would go right this year; he would make goddamned sure of it.
He had learned to climb and had trained himself in mountain
survival techniques. He was tougher now, prepared for
anything. There would be no more disasters.

A sudden movement of air made Gordon's head whirl
around.

The dog, he remembered, too late, as the animal struck him
full force in the ribs, hurling him to the dirt. Its clicking jaws
snapped shut on his calf. Where the devil was Ted? Gordon
kicked and struggled but could not break free. The teeth were
hot points of pain, working their way through the denim of
his jeans. He faked a dodge, throwing the dog off balance, and
heaved himself beyond the reach of the tether.

An old mining pick lay against the side of Ted's cabin. Before
Gordon knew it, the heavy maple shank was in his hands. He

felt a wave of righteous energy as he turned back to the snarling animal.

That's right, do it. Great way to start off the season, Gordon.

He dropped the pick, ashamed of himself, and examined his wound. *Christ, the bite didn't even break the skin.* He had overreacted. The sound of a faraway freight train began to rumble in the back of Gordon's brain, making his teeth chatter.

He hadn't really wanted to use the mining pick on the dog, to chop open its underbelly. He didn't want to watch its innards spill out.

He'd never meant any harm to anyone.

2

Del

Del Albright led a hunting party into the dark tangled pine forest surrounding Wolf Gulch. The boys were armed with hatchets, knives, and an assortment of makeshift weapons. They would stalk a rabbit or a squirrel to test their prowess as trackers.

Del glanced over his shoulder. *These guys would follow me anywhere,* he thought proudly. In the junglelike heat they had doffed their shirts, and Del admired the angry red slashes the brambles had inflicted on their arms and backs. Now the boys looked like real hunters.

A bold squawk from overhead startled Del. Something blue dive-bombed him and swooped ahead into the bushes.

"Scrub jay!" shouted Steve Haines, a gaunt, almost skeletal kid.

Del heard a whistling sound. Haines's firewood hatchet flew past his ear and slammed into a conifer with a resounding *whish-shunk.*

Del whirled around. "Hey! Don't *ever* throw your hatchet when there's a guy in front of you."

"Nice going, Haines," Miles Brummel said. He was a stocky thirteen-year-old with a fat neck and a flattop.

"I just wanted to see if it would stick in the tree," Haines admitted, blushing.

Del rolled his eyes. "When are you going to learn to *think* before you act, Haines? I swear."

A stranger might have taken him for a father rebuking his errant son. Del knew he did not look much like a teenager. "An overgrown weed," he liked to call himself. With his height—six-foot-four—his powerful physique, and his summer mustache, he could have passed for twenty-five. Del enjoyed the authority his size automatically bestowed on him. On the first day of camp, everyone had thought he was a counselor. Some of the little kids probably still did.

He heard gravel churning in the distance and cocked his head. "Car coming in."

"Probably the new kid," Haines commented. "How come he's late, anyway?"

"So what if he's late," Del said.

"He's probably some poor slob who can't get his act together," Miles muttered.

"I'm sure he's perfectly okay." Del gave him a hard look. "Don't get any ideas, Miles."

Del led them jogging to the dirt road in time to watch a station wagon approaching. A tense man in a business suit was hunched over the steering wheel. Next to him sat a lean, defiant boy wearing a leather cap. He had slicked-back hair and sharp hawklike features. The kid gave Del a hard glance before the wagon accelerated around a bend into camp.

A brindle-colored rabbit suddenly skittered across the road and bounded into the brush.

"Rabbit!" Haines cried, darting after it.

Curious about the new boy, Del left the others and cut back through the woods. As he neared the parking lot, he overheard voices and hunched down, peering through the foliage.

Mr. Dugan, the camp director, was conversing with the new kid's father. The boy was gone, probably taking his gear to his cabin. Del could only make out bits and pieces of the conversation.

"Then what *is* wrong with Kyle, Mr. Cody?" Mr. Dugan asked. The camp director was a jovial prep school principal with cotton candy hair and rheumy blue eyes that always looked distracted.

"Terrible tragedy," Mr. Cody said, shaking his head. He began angrily chiseling bird droppings off his station wagon with a piece of bark. "... His older brother, Marshall," he continued. "You know, disturbed. He drowned in ..."

Del strained forward with rapt attention, trying to catch every word. Taking a risk, he inched a few paces into the cabin clearing.

"... Kyle feels responsible. He never got over the accident. But the time has come for him to get past it. That's why we're here."

"Yes, well, it certainly must have been traumatic for him," Mr. Dugan said.

"I expect the best from Kyle—top performance—and I want him to *have* the best. But not the easy way." Mr. Cody eyed the upthrust Sierra rim appraisingly. "Your brochure says you have a wilderness survival program. Something to separate the strong from the weak."

Mr. Dugan nodded, producing a broad P.R. smile. "You bet we do. To start off with is the Wolf Gulch Ordeal. It's a rather challenging overnight hike that instills a sense of self-reliance in the campers, a respect for Mother Nature—"

"Save your sales pitch," Mr. Cody interrupted. "I sent the kid here to have his balls busted a little. He needs a challenge. Something to bring him out of himself."

Mr. Dugan nodded, looking slightly uneasy. "I'm sure Kyle will be happy here."

"I don't care if he's happy—I want him to learn the goddamned *rules*," Mr. Cody said urgently.

"Yes, of course. The rules of proper conduct."

"No, I'm talking about the rules of the real world, Mr. Dugan. Let's face it, for better or worse, society is success-oriented: Life is *war*, life is *winning*. Survival of the fittest. That's the way it's always been."

3

Kyle

A lone, Kyle Cody dumped his duffel bag in the dank cabin, then stormed into the deep, late afternoon shadows of the conifer wood.

I hate this place.

He had no reason to speak to anyone. He did not want to sign in for chores or go to dinner. He did not want to attend campfire for announcements and folk songs. His father had forced him to come to Wolf Gulch; Kyle had never wanted it. All he wanted now was to be left alone.

Maybe I'll just start walking and never come back. Maybe I'll go so far they'll never find me.

Mercifully, the trail was empty. Kyle crept noiselessly past the ancient mine shaft and outbuildings, pleased with his stealth. He could glide through the forest like an Indian scout, silent and invisible. In a graceful bound, he leapt over a small ravine. The sounds of the forest grew louder, more daring: bushes creaked, pine boughs hissed. Crickets cheeped in unison and the whole woods seemed to hum in a low, vibrating chorus of crepitations. Kyle sucked in a lungful of resiny air and nearly smiled, savoring his solitude. He imagined himself a lone forest dweller living off the land, dependent on no one: a mountain man. An owl hooted eerily and he glanced up. The stark sun-washed hulk of the Sierras caught his eye through the trees.

Kyle halted before a towering fir whose branches dipped thickly to the ground. Parting the boughs, he ducked down and crawled into the space between the ground and the fan of trunk branches. The dark tree-cave smelled of damp pine needles.

Kyle sat cross-legged, instantly at ease. Back home, he had a tree sanctuary like this in the empty lot next door. It was his special, secret place for finding the solace only solitude could bring.

He leaned against the trunk and his hair stuck to the bark, fastening him to the tree. He smiled. Now he was part of that tree, part of the forest, responsible for nothing more than just existing.

A sparky squirrel darted into Kyle's sanctuary with a pinecone in its mouth. It gave him a beady stare before scurrying under the wall of boughs. Kyle sighed and crawled wearily back into the outer world. He left the path, bushwhacking through the undergrowth to avoid a chance encounter with other campers.

Soon he heard the murmur of lapping water and emerged on the short mud beach of Lake Sequoia. It was chalky blue and scalloped by wind-driven wavelets. On the point, Wolf Gulch campers were diving off a pier and swimming to the float a hundred feet offshore.

Turning away, Kyle stumbled over a half-buried tree stump, pulling it from the mud with his foot. Spidery white bugs scuttled out of the water-filled hole. He peered into the cavity.

A drowning face gaped up at him, bloated and turning purple—a living death mask. From its open mouth belched a final rush of bubbles. The bulging eyes begged for it to be over,

Kyle jerked away, shaken. He looked into the hole again and saw his own face, a harmless reflection distorted in the sinkhole. But the image had resembled *another* face much like his own—*a* face he did not want to see. Trembling, Kyle wiped sweatbeads from his brow and snatched another look into the cavity.

A massive visage grinned up from behind his reflection. He recoiled with a gasp and wheeled around.

A tall, powerfully built figure loomed over Kyle, laughing at his fright. The man had friendly, intelligent eyes, and his nose was peeling from sunburn. "Didn't you hear me yelling, Kyle?"

Caught off guard, Kyle shook his head. The man already knew his name; he must be a counselor.

"Name's Del." He grabbed Kyle's hand and pumped it vigorously. "Your presence is cordially requested at the canoe dock."

"What for?"

"Come on, the guys are waiting for us. Let's haul ass."

Kyle reluctantly complied; he couldn't blatantly disobey a counselor. They plodded up the beach, mud sucking at their sneakers.

Two boys were waiting for them on a dock where the canoes were moored. They scrutinized Kyle with curious invading eyes. He felt himself tense up. He did not want to be here.

"What is this?" Kyle said. "I don't need a canoe lesson."

"We're going to canoe-*joust*," Del announced with a grand gesture, as though it were an Olympic sporting event.

"Are you a counselor?" Kyle demanded.

Del shook his head with a grin.

"How old are you?"

"Fifteen," Del admitted proudly. "Did that fake you out?"

"*Fifteen?* Shit." Kyle felt a wave of anger. They were the same age. He'd been duped.

Del introduced him to the other two campers, Miles Brummel and Steve Haines. Del might have been only fifteen but he wielded the commanding presence of an adult.

"How come you're late?" Miles inquired with a probing, sideways glance, as though lateness were a crime. This kind of boxed-in situation was exactly why Kyle had wanted to be left alone.

"My dad wanted me at Outward Bound," Kyle explained in a stiff tone. "He applied too late. I couldn't get in. Wolf Gulch still had room."

"I'll bet it did," Miles said with a snort. "Outward Bound's for pukes."

"Hey, I didn't ask to go anywhere."

"You're not a puke, are you, Kyle?" Miles taunted.

"Eat shit," Kyle mumbled, glaring at the whitewashed boards of the dock.

"Okay, the rules are simple," Del said briskly. He pointed at two curtain rods lying on the dock, a boxing glove bound to each end with duct tape. "Each jouster tries to knock the other out of his canoe. Lose your canoe and you lose the game."

Kyle was handed an oar and assigned to the stern of Del's

canoe. He hesitated, though he seemed to have no choice in the matter. *You don't back down from challenges, son,* Dad would say. It was too late to back down now anyway. Kyle paddled with Del into deep water, ruminating over the tense father-and-son canoe trips Dad had insisted they take together every year.

He caught Del staring at him. "Don't let Miles get to you," Del said.

"I'm not."

"His parents are jet-setters. They dump him at a new camp every summer while they fly off to some cushy vacation."

"Why a new camp every summer?"

Del laughed. "No place'll ever take him back."

The contest began amid much splashing and shouting, the enemy canoe bearing down on them at a fast clip. Bare-chested and glistening with spray, Del made ferocious war-whoops from the prow, brandishing his curtain rod, feet braced inside the gunwales. Kyle likened him to Conan the Barbarian: huge and invincible, demanding respect.

Kyle grimly guided their canoe in a series of whippy, unpredictable turns and deceptive dodges, neatly outwitting the enemy. A risky collision-course attack finally forced Miles and Haines to veer off sharply. Their canoe capsized, dumping them into the drink.

"All *right?'* Del cheered. "You did it, you old bandit."

"I told you I didn't need canoe lessons."

"Come on, this calls for a celebration," Del insisted after they returned the canoes to the dock and he sent Miles and Haines back to camp. He produced a smuggled bottle of blackberry brandy from his day pack and leapt onto the boathouse roof. Kyle joined him reluctantly. Del raised the flask in an effusive toast.

"To the winning team. We really showed them, didn't we?"

Kyle shrugged and took a long swig. The sweet syrupy liquid burned all the way to his belly.

Del gazed up at the mountains like a grandee admiring his

domain. "So what do you think?" he asked. "Is this just fucking incredible or what?"

"I guess."

"Wouldn't it be a gas to be way up there?" Del pointed up at the Sierras. "Just you and me against the elements!"

Kyle pondered this, recalling his own fantasy of living off the land. Del would make one hell of a mountain man: dependable, solid, confident. In a crisis, Del could probably pull them through anything.

"So what about it, bro?" Del gave him a playful punch on the arm. "Are we friends now or what?"

Kyle hesitated. No one had ever asked him for friendship so bluntly before. Finally, he nodded.

Del raised the bottle. "To comrades-in-arms, then. Blood brothers."

Blood brothers.

Kyle froze. His throat closed off. His mouth went dry and cottony.

The drowning face—the hands holding it down—the underwater scream.

His heart beat so fast he thought it would jackhammer its way out of his chest.

"Blood brothers," he finally managed to croak.

4

Gordon

Gordon sat alone in the campfire circle, watching the sun settle behind the Sierra crest. The campers and other counselors were at dinner, but Gordon had no appetite. Tomorrow was the first day of the Wolf Gulch Ordeal.

A hush fell over the glen, save for the hiss of the wind through the pines and the chittering of a roosting rock wren. After a week of hollering campers and yappy counselors, Gordon took comfort in the absence of human sound. He drew in deep lungfuls of the night air perfumed by the scent of pine needles. The twilight chill registered as he exhaled.

Night fell swiftly. Gordon put a match to the kindling and pitchwood he had laid in tepee fashion. He stared at the spreading flame with satisfaction. It was a pity that fire-building had become a lost art in today's era of charcoal briquets and starter fluid.

Within minutes the bonfire crackled effortlessly. But the leaping flames did little to ward off the pervading gloom of the woods. To Gordon, The Wilds radiated a certain malevolence in the eerie moonglow—a nearly palpable force.

Perfect night for a scary story, Gordon mused, waxing macabre. He needed something to keep the kids from straggling tomorrow. How about Cal Wolcroft? No, the thought made his skin crawl. The campers and most of the staff were new this year; probably only a few counselors knew about the Wolcroft incident and the mysterious, grotesque circumstances of his death. So far, no one had mentioned it.

The memory of Wolcroft's mutilated body brought back

images of the grisly traffic films Gordon had used to scare his students into defensive driving. His stint as driving instructor at the Milwaukee Day School had lasted two years. Classes four afternoons a week and summers at Wolf Gulch had paid his bills, leaving ample time for his writing. Five years earlier, Gordon had forsaken his doctoral studies in psychology to devote himself entirely to his book about lucid dreaming. But he still hadn't been able to get a hook on those early chapters.

Lucid dreaming—the ability to become fully conscious and manipulate the outcome of the dream. If people could learn to control their dream life, Gordon believed, they could change their waking life for the better. He had been a lucid dreamer since he was seven. If a monster was chasing him, he could recognize that he was dreaming, redirect the dream, face down the ogre, and finally tame or destroy it. Lucid dreaming was a way to bridge the gap between the conscious and unconscious.

After years of labor, feeling full of naive optimism, Gordon had showed his notes for the proposed book to an old psychology prof. "Psychobabble," his mentor had called it. "Much too esoteric for the public at large. It's not even backed up with clinical data. I suggest, Gordon, that you set your sights on writing something you're better equipped to handle." Gordon took the criticism as a slap in the face.

"Guess you're an iggerant just like the old man," Dad had commented with a snicker when he heard about the put-down. *"Wouldn't it be a kick in the ass—you ending up pushing a broom? Like father, like son, right?"*

Iggerant was one of his father's many mispronunciations; Gordon was never sure which ones were due to Dad's drinking and which were deliberate. The man enjoyed needling Gordon with his illiterate act.

Before Dad's death of stomach cancer last year, Gordon used to daydream about the glowing reviews his book would receive in *The New York Times* and *Newsweek*. He would march downstairs to the school boiler room where Dad—"Pop" Hollos, to his friends—had worked for thirty years. The hot and humid dungeon stank of petroleum gas and body odor. Gordon would simply proffer a folded newspaper.

"What's this?" Dad would raise his eyebrows until the ruddy skin on his forehead wrinkled into deep grooves. He wouldn't touch the paper.

"*Come on, Dad, it's* The New York Times."

"*You know I won't read that hoity-toity rag.*"

"*But they've reviewed my book!*"

Gordon liked to imagine that Dad would scan the review and embrace him in a huge bear hug. But that wouldn't have been like Pop Hollos, professional cynic. He had a nose-thumbing reputation to live up to as the only local janitor with a master's degree. His candy-coated, acerbic wit masked a bitter resentment against anyone who had made something of himself. Dad was an alcoholic, a have-not who would never forgive the haves.

"*Oh really,* The New York Times?" Dad might have said, his face a study of wide-eyed, exaggerated wonder. "*I* am *impressed.*" That old sarcasm was never far beneath the surface. "*What did you do to get this printed, Gordo, slip someone a C-note?*" Pop Hollos would have guffawed in peals of bitter mirth before breaking down into his hacking, asthmatic cough. He had destroyed Gordon's dreams with the same perverse delight he had taken in sabotaging his own life.

Gordon sighed and glanced up the path. The campers would be coming any time now.

He reflected that he still might be running those driver's-ed films for fifteen-year-olds, if it hadn't been for the Billy Robin incident. After what had happened, he couldn't blame the Milwaukee Day School headmaster for letting him go.

Billy Robin had had it in for him. The hyper, fast-talking junior was the class cut-up who had never failed at anything in his life. But Gordon had flunked him for cutting too many classes, forcing him to repeat the course. He'd made himself an enemy.

Billy delighted in finding ways to disrupt Gordon's class. He finally went too far the day Gordon gave his standard speech on drunk driving. This was always Gordon's favorite lecture. For once the kids were paying attention, genuinely curious to know how much they could drink and still pass the breath test.

Then Billy started kicking his foot loudly against the stanchion of his desk: *tap-tap-tap*. The kid had an innate talent for needling irritation.

"Cut that out, Billy. Do not jiggle," Gordon said.

A few other students tittered and joined in with that incessant *tap-tap-tap*.

"Now that's enough."

The room settled into mocking silence. Why didn't the others see through Billy's antics—that he couldn't stand anyone else to be the center of attention?

"Got a screw loose," Billy whispered, just loud enough to be audible. Somebody giggled.

I will not lose control of this classroom to an adolescent.

"About the breath tests," Gordon continued, undaunted. "The general rule for one drink an hour, say a can of beer, is directly proportional to—"

"Hell, I can suck up a six-pack and drive *better* than I can sober," Billy announced, mimicking a drunk.

Gordon tapped the top of his desk with his chalk. "Get up here, Billy."

"Me?" Billy's eyes narrowed to slits.

"Up to the front of the room, Mr. Man. Right now."

Billy grinned and swaggered up the aisle. "What's the prob? Just trying to contribute to the class discussion."

Gordon gave him a sizzling glare. "Were you drinking before class, Billy?"

"No, I was boffing Marsha Gottfried in the can."

A few male students chuckled and jeered.

"You mean you were smoking grass in the can. I can smell it on you."

The boy's grin widened. "Excuse me, *sir*, that stuff's illegal."

The way Billy said *sir* was like a slap in the face. Gordon could see Billy a year from now, joyriding in a fast car, zoned out on crack. There would be a bloody aftermath, dismembered bodies strewn across a median strip. Unless he could get through to the boy, Gordon felt those deaths would be on his shoulders.

"Look, I know you don't give a damn about driver's ed, Billy.

But this is serious stuff—it's important. *Comprende?*"

"*Sí, señor.* Can I go back to my seat now?"

"No. Now listen to me, Billy. Drugs and alcohol give a false sense of power. Sure, you might think you're more capable at the wheel after a few tokes or drinks, but clinical tests show just the opposite."

Billy fidgeted and tapped his foot restlessly. Gordon noticed a flask-shaped bulge in the front pocket of the boy's jeans.

"What's that in your pocket, Billy?"

Billy blinked. "Prescription cough medicine."

"Hey, can I have a jolt, Bill?" somebody said with a chortle. "My throat hurts."

"Shut up," Gordon snapped. He looked Billy square in the eye. "That bulge is a bottle, isn't it?"

"No, I'm just *happy* to see you," Billy quipped.

"Let's have it."

"Why don't you frisk me, *Mr. Man?* I'll bet you like feeling up young bucks, don't you?"

"That's enough." Gordon blushed angrily. "Now hand it over."

"Take it."

Billy didn't budge an inch. The classroom fell silent, everyone waiting for Gordon to make the next move.

Gordon faltered, uneasy. He glanced up at the wall clock and saw that class was almost over. "All right … class dismissed." Everyone bolted to their feet. "*You* stay put, Billy."

The students piled out, a few lingering behind to see what would happen. It was a standoff. Billy stood in a pose of frozen belligerence, a cocky smile on his face. For all Gordon knew, the boy could be carrying a weapon. Despite his mounting rage, Gordon couldn't risk it. He averted his gaze.

"I'm going to have to report this, Billy."

"You do that." Billy turned and walked out, cool as could be.

Gordon sought refuge in the men's room and tried to collect himself.

You really blew it this time, you poor stupid iggerant! *How are you ever going to face that class again?*

He wasn't just furious, he was humiliated. Once again, Billy had gotten the better of him. Once again, somebody had refused to take Gordon seriously. If it wasn't Pop Hollos or his old psychology prof, it was a sixteen-year-old punk!

Gordon balled his hand into a fist and slammed it against the cinder-block wall. The skin on his knuckles split open. He stared at his fingers as if he'd never seen blood before.

Then he heard a familiar sound: *tap-tap-tap*, Billy Robin was leaning against a toilet stall, foot-tapping the partition, a shrewd grin on his face.

"Lighten up, Mr. Man," Billy said. "Shit happens, you know?" He took a joint from his pocket. "Got a light?"

Gordon let loose a snarl of outrage. He grabbed Billy by the shoulders, smearing the boy's shirt with the blood from his own knuckles.

"Do *not* jiggle!" he shouted, shoving the boy against the steel partition. Billy's face turned white and he tried to break away. Gordon shook him like a terrier with a rat, Billy's head bouncing and slamming against the wall. "Do *not* jiggle!"

"If there hadn't been that blood all over his shirt, Gordon, I might have gotten the committee to understand," the headmaster had confided the following day. *"I really hate to let you go like this."*

Whispering voices drew Gordon from his reverie. Two nine-year-old campers—Marcus Squier, as skinny as a rain gutter, and Lissa Knauf, a short, squat girl with cropped red hair—had already taken seats on the benches. Gordon hadn't even heard them enter the fire circle.

Other kids arrived, chattering among themselves. Some darted quick glances at Gordon, no doubt wondering why he had skipped supper. He knew he was both feared and admired at Wolf Gulch. *You don't mess with Gordon,* they probably whispered to each other. He rather liked the image of himself as the tough, silent maverick, the lone wolf.

Kyle Cody sat down in the back row and tossed Gordon a flinty glance. Here was a boy who was hard to read. His cool streetwise air and leather cap suggested a certain worldly wisdom, as if there was little he hadn't seen in life. The other kids avoided Kyle, but he didn't seem to care. Drawn to the boy,

Gordon could see himself in Kyle at fifteen. *Fifteen!* God, what a vulnerable, volatile age that was, when peer pressure and popularity held mighty sway over all.

Del Albright and his girlfriend, Gillian Malloy, took their seats. Gillian was a quiet fifteen-year-old with long blonde hair and an almost frightening beauty. She was devoted to Del and never took her eyes off him. Gordon wondered whether she even had a will of her own.

The last few stragglers arrived with the other counselors. The camp director, Jerry Dugan, strode into the campfire circle with tall, athletic-looking Cindy Blaisdell, the new female counselor.

Jerry scratched his balding pate and cleared his throat. "All right, chuckleheads, may I have your kind attention, please? Tomorrow, as you all know, we tackle the Wolf Gulch Ordeal. It's a real tradition around here! Now, unfortunately, only twelve of you are coming. I'm sure the rest of you already know your parents wouldn't sign the releases." Several campers groaned.

Jerry shrugged his shoulders in a what-can-I-do-about-it gesture. "Sorry. Now for you trekkers, wake-up call is at five thirty. Cindy was counting on going up with us, but she's still feeling under the weather. So you'll have only Gordon and myself to put up with.

"The trailhead starts at a place called Foxtail Meadow. We'll have a full day's march into The Wilds and camp at nine thousand feet on the shores of Lost Lake. If we run into any bad weather, there're a couple of abandoned prospectors' cabins. Next morning, we climb another thousand feet to Skyline Fireroad, where the bus picks us up at sundown."

Jerry hiked up his safari shorts and plopped himself down on a stump. Gordon heard his white, gnarly knees pop.

"We're talking about real, untouched wilderness up there," the camp director continued. "No tourists, no beer cans. God's country!"

"That means there won't be anyone around to find any campers dumb enough to lose their way," Gordon cut in.

Jerry nodded. "Thank goodness we'll have Gordon up there as our guide," he said with a twinkle in his eye. "Gordon's got tons of mountaineering experience under his belt and he really knows the terrain. Isn't that right, old boy?"

Gordon managed to nod dutifully, jaw working. He didn't care much for this nature-walk approach to The Wilds. Jerry was a greenhorn; he lacked the experience needed for the high country. He had no idea how bad it could get in The Wilds.

"Has anyone here ever done any mountain hiking?" Gordon asked.

Gillian was the only one to raise her hand. "I'm in the Sierra Club back home in Boulder. I mean, my family is. We hike the Rockies sometimes."

"The Sierra Club, okay," Gordon said, impressed.

"Mr. Dugan, are we going to be hiking in the snow?" Jennifer Zurich asked. She was a high-spirited eleven-year-old tomboy with flashing eyes.

"Gordon?" Jerry said, deferring to Gordon's expertise with a wave of his hand.

"Most of the snow left this time of year is up on the summits," Gordon replied. "We won't be climbing anywhere near that high."

"What about man-eating animals?" Jennifer said.

"Oh, you might see a brown bear or a mountain lion if you're lucky. But they don't attack people, Jennifer. Not unless you corner them. Tomorrow night I'll show you how to hang your food packs in the trees to keep the bears away."

Gordon turned to Jerry. "What kind of weather is the National Weather Service predicting? You called them, I hope."

Jerry nodded. "For tomorrow they're expecting clear skies and seventy-five degrees—top-drawer conditions, eh?"

"Sounds good."

"Seems there might be a little localized mountain weather the next day," Jerry said. "Some cloud cover, maybe rain."

"Rain?" Miles moaned.

"Make sure you bring your ponchos, everybody."

"Maybe we ought to postpone the hike for a couple of days," Gordon said.

Jerry shook his head. "That would interfere with the swim meet." He smiled. "Besides, what's the Wolf Gulch Ordeal without a hardship or two?"

The moon faded and brightened with the passage of clouds, like a guttering candle.

"Let's just say you get lost," Jerry considered out loud with a bemused air, as if in a game. "Let's say you're marooned up in The Wilds. What's the most important thing to bring with you?"

"Survival gear, right?" Del said.

"A hunting knife or a hatchet," Gillian suggested.

"Wrong," Gordon broke in harshly. "Your *brain's* your best survival gear." He rose to his feet, pacing around the fire to emphasize his words. "I don't think any of you greenhorns realize that we all live in a fragile comfort zone. Even here at camp. Lower the temperature a little, take away your creature comforts, and any us can die if we're not prepared.

"Let's say you're up hiking in The Wilds and you get your feet wet in a creek. And say a storm's moving in. With more experience, you might have recognized the thick stratocumulus thunderheads on the horizon and had time to prepare a shelter. But you didn't, and now it's too late.

"The wind picks up. Suddenly you can't stop shivering. You're having hallucinations: *fata morgana*, they're called. Mental mirages, like an oasis in the desert. You've got hypothermia—exposure—the killer of the unprepared. At home, you'd go inside and turn up the thermostat or maybe take a hot bath. Up there you don't have any of those options. You're vulnerable. You've got to find shelter and warmth, and find it fast." He tapped the side of his head meaningfully. "Unless that survival gear upstairs is in high gear and knows what to do, you're in deep trouble."

The campers eyed him with fearful reverence, soaking up every word.

"Very interesting," Jerry remarked hurriedly. "Thank the good Lord we won't have *that* to contend with. We'll have plenty of warm clothes and food in our backpacks."

"Yes, but you have to anticipate emergencies," Gordon insisted. "Anything can happen. Don't forget what happened to the Donner Party." He paused for effect. "You do know about the Donner Party, don't you, kids?"

"Donner and Blitzen?" Jennifer asked. Miles guffawed.

"You think that's *funny*, Miles?" Gordon said. "The Donners were pioneers who didn't anticipate their emergency. They were stranded for a whole winter and ran out of food. And there weren't any rescue helicopters in the nineteenth century. The Donners had to eat their dead to stay alive."

"You mean like cannibals?" Lonny Brown said, a scruffy, buck-toothed little boy whose eyes had gone wide with alarm.

"Sure," Del said. "Just like those guys whose plane went down in the Andes. The soccer team."

"There's more to the story, though. They say one Donner Party survivor didn't lose a pound all winter. A big, strapping German fellow. He developed quite a taste for human flesh, it seems. Children in particular."

"Now Gordon," Jerry interrupted, turning to the campers, "I think it's high time we all—"

"That Donner Man was always hungry," Gordon went on. "Some say he still stalks The Wilds, shuffling through the maze of trails up there, hunting for his next meal." His voice rose an octave, giving the kids a start: *"So you people better damn well stick together on the trail!"*

"Gordon!" Jerry snapped. "That's quite enough now."

"Relax, will you? I need to make a point here." Didn't Jerry understand? Gordon had to warn these kids about The Wilds— scare the bejesus out of them any way he could.

The wind picked up, bending the conifers over on themselves, and they moaned back at The Wilds in a keen rising whine. The moonlit Sierras glowed so fiercely that their radiance seemed to shine from within.

5

Kyle

After campfire, while the counselors occupied themselves with preparations for the Ordeal, Del organized a game of capture the flag. The campers assembled on the baseball diamond, a dark arena of stubby Sierra grass illuminated by a center field bonfire. Kyle stood away from the others. Del was running things as usual, he observed coolly.

"Listen up, everybody," Del announced through cupped hands. "Gillian and I are the captains tonight."

"Unfair!" The protest had come from Page Montcrieff, a frail but feisty little boy with a stubborn cowlick, whom Del had christened "the Professor." He was Wolf Gulch's youngest camper. "You two were captains last night," Page said. "That's discrimination against the masses."

"Whatever you say, Page," Del said with an easy laugh, towering over him. "Why don't you and me be captains? Gillian won't mind."

Page hesitated. "I wasn't suggesting that."

Nothing more needed to be said. Del always knew what to say and how to make people answer to his beck and call. It seemed almost unconscionable to Kyle how everything came so easily to Del, as if he were born to be favored. The kid was the star camper, and his being captain was an automatic assumption. After all, so Kyle had heard, he was president of his class, captain of the soccer team, editor of the yearbook—the perfect teen-ager, sailing straight through life without a single hitch.

Dad would love to have a son like that, the son of a bitch.

Kyle doubted he could ever measure up to such standards. He would never be elected captain of a team, nor did he want to be.

"Kyle," Del said, breaking his train of thought, "you're on my team. And I want Miles, Haines—"

"Give me a break, Del," Gillian cut in. "You're taking all the big kids."

"Okay, then you get Haines and Frank," Del decided, gesturing at older camper Frank Navit, a cop's son with the hefty build of a defensive end. "I'll take Lewis," Del added.

Lewis Borwosky, a fragile youth with a bookish face, grinned and flexed his tiny muscles. "Brains over brawn, jock," he told Frank.

The teams split off to opposite sides of the first base line. Del's team huddled around him. He traced his finger on a patch of dirt, sketching an elaborate strategy to psych out the other team. Kyle lingered on the outskirts of the huddle and methodically kicked a hole in the grass with his shoe. Again, almost against his will, he thought of his father.

I want you on the winning team, son. Now make me proud.

—Fuck you.

Kyle stared across the first base line at Gillian, overseeing the enemy team. She was flawlessly dressed in Benetton casuals, he noted snidely. Her blonde hair fluttered in the night breeze, fashion-plate perfect. She smiled in Kyle's direction. He turned away self-consciously.

"Okay, six of you will form an offensive phalanx to zero in on our objective," Del told the group, trying to sound like General Patton. The enemy flag had been planted under the water tower at the other end of camp. "Synchronize your watches to nine o'clock. We'll regroup at the boathouse and launch our blitzkrieg."

Lewis was assigned to guard the team's flag, anchored on the pitcher's mound. "If the enemy gets too close," Del told him, "stuff the flag up your shirt. Just say somebody already captured it."

"What if they don't believe me?" Lewis said.

"Just use your head."

A dark projectile suddenly whizzed past and exploded a few feet away. The terrific report echoed off the faraway barricade of The Wilds. Kyle fell back, his ears ringing.

"Outstanding!" Miles roared, emerging from the woods holding a box of firecrackers. "What's a war without artillery?" With *baa*-like spates of frenetic laughter, he quickly passed out firecrackers to the others.

"You're going to get us all in hot water with those things," Frank warned. "That's a misdemeanor under local law. My dad's a cop, you know."

"Blow it out your ass," Miles said.

"That's a physical impossibility, Miles," Page noted.

"Save it, Professor, game's on," Del said.

He signaled for the maneuvers to begin, then grabbed Kyle. "Keep with me!" he whispered, and darted into the foggy woods.

Kyle followed, zigzagging around boulders and vine-covered tree trunks, straining to match Del's pace. From behind came a staccato of booming firecrackers. Dazzling blue-white flashes blinded him. Through the foliage, Kyle caught a glimpse of the rest of the team advancing in a V-shaped attack phalanx. Acrid smoke clouds billowed across the path, prickling his nostrils, obscuring his view of the campers running helter-skelter across the field.

Nearby, a child's tinny voice shrieked in pure terror: "Don't hurt me! Don't hurt me!"

Someone let loose a war-whoop that sounded more animal than human, a savage yammering that gave Kyle the willies. *This must be what war is like*, he thought, running like a deer flushed into flight. A camper could really get hurt here. He wished Gordon would step in and put a stop to it.

A body collided with Kyle, knocking him to the ground. He bounded to his feet and ran to catch up, but Del had sprinted out of sight. The forest was strewn with "casualties"—tagged teammates playing dead on the ground, some of them giggling and joking. Kyle was in enemy territory now.

An unseen assailant suddenly jabbed him in the small of his back. He yelped and fell forward into a heap of pine needles.

Turning, he recognized Gillian through the smoke and rose to his feet. She grinned in triumph.

"Hey, you can't move, you're dead!" she cried.

"I'm not even wounded. You'll have to do better than that."

"Oh yeah?"

Gillian tackled him. The two of them rolled in the duff, tussling like bear cubs.

"Hey, no tickling!" Kyle protested. For the first time since arriving at camp, he let loose an uninhibited chuckle.

"You're dead, you're dead!" Gillian said with a laugh.

Suddenly, from somewhere, a voice shouted, "*Hey!*"

A hand caught Kyle's shoulder. Del loomed over them like a giant, out of breath. Kyle and Gillian immediately moved apart.

"You're free, Kyle," Del barked, taking off again. "Keep up with me this time."

Kyle abandoned Gillian and hurried after his friend. They ran to the parking lot behind the supply shed. The continuous musketry of firecrackers punctuated the silence of the woods. Del hopped aboard the Wolf Gulch bus.

"Jeez, what're you going to do, hot-wire it?" Kyle said.

"I'll go one better." Del groped behind the sun visor, produced a key, and handed it to Kyle with a grin. "Fire this baby up."

"You got to be shitting me," Kyle said. "What about the blitzkrieg?"

"That was just a cover. Don't worry, I have a plan."

"Isn't this cheating?"

"Hey, all's fair in love and war. Now go ahead, bro, crank it."

Kyle just stared at him.

"You *do* know how to drive a stick, don't you?"

"Sure," Kyle admitted. "But—"

"Come on, then," Del urged. "Are we in this together or what?"

Kyle tilted his head, suspicious. "You want *me* to be the one who gets into trouble."

"No way, man. Okay, okay … I don't know how to drive."

Kyle snickered, half-relieved by Del's confession. Mustering his nerve, he turned the ignition key. The engine rumbled to life. He flicked on the lights. The gears protested loudly as he shifted into first.

"Watch the noise," Del warned.

With a jarring lurch the bus trundled forward and bounced down a two-wheel track into the woods. Kyle gripped the giant wheel, adjusting to the wide steering.

"Douse those headlights," Del ordered, leaning halfway out the open door.

Kyle complied, following the moonlit road, proud that he could handle such a huge vehicle. He savored the lumbering power of its motion, the high riding. *Next stop, Sierra crest. Mean machine, comin' through!* He was beginning to enjoy this.

"Look *out!*"

Del lunged and caught the wheel, yanking it away from Kyle, forcing the bus off the side of the trail. Kyle slammed the brake pedal to the floor. The vehicle careened up on two wheels, nearly flipping over, and slammed to a halt in a rutted ditch.

"Way to go, asshole!" Del shouted. "You almost nailed Page!"

"What are you talking about?"

Del pointed into the woods and Kyle caught sight of the silhouette of a small, retreating figure with a cowlick. "He crossed right in front of you!"

"I didn't see him!" Trembling, Kyle wrenched the ignition key. The engine wouldn't catch. "I didn't see him."

"You better hope he doesn't rat on us."

Kyle pumped the accelerator as if he were stomping a small animal to death. The odor of gasoline wafted up.

"Great. Now you've flooded her," Del said.

"Just give me a minute."

Del leaped out of the bus. "We don't *have* a minute. Come on. And bring that flashlight."

Ears burning, Kyle jumped out and followed. They jogged another hundred yards until the outline of the water tower emerged from the fog.

Del turned, eyes on the enemy flag. "If we get separated, I'll wait for you in the arroyo."

Kyle nodded dumbly.

Frank was guarding the enemy flag beneath the tower. On

Del's instructions, Kyle waved the flashlight at him, acting as the decoy.

"Hey, Frank! I hear your mom sucks police dog dicks!" The big burly kid came scrambling after Kyle. At the same time, Del snatched the flag with a magician's speed and disappeared into the woods.

"Suck *this*, pussy!" Frank cried, tagging Kyle with a shove that sent him reeling into a bush.

"Thanks for the memory, pal." Kyle jumped to his feet with a gleeful grin and took off at a zigzagging clip.

"Hey, you can't do that, you're tagged," Frank protested as Kyle dashed into the woods. "Cheater!"

Del was waiting for him in the foggy, rock-littered arroyo. "We did it," he cheered in a barely restrained whisper, waving the flag.

"The counselors are going to wonder about the bus," Kyle said flatly. "You won't tell them anything, will you?"

"Don't be stupid."

The rutted up-and-down trail forced them to walk in single file. Kyle led the way with the flashlight He stopped suddenly and turned to Del.

"Let me carry the flag."

"No way."

"Why not? I thought we were in this together."

Del planted his hands on his hips. "The plan was *my* idea and *I* got the flag. You got yourself tagged by a girl and I had to come back and rescue you."

"Shut up."

"Then you would have killed Page if I hadn't grabbed the wheel. You almost blew it Kyle, let's face it."

"I said *shut up!*"

"You should have just done it right, that's all."

"Don't tell me what to do. You're *not* my fucking father!" Kyle glared at him, wanting to snatch away the flag and shred it to bits. He turned and quickly walked away.

The fog grew thicker, impenetrable.

"I can't see a thing," Del piped up from behind. "Let me know if there's a rock or something."

Kyle did not answer.

The going was treacherous. He could hear Del behind him, grunting his way over the tree branches and boulder debris. Kyle barked his shin but felt nothing. His limbs were heavy and wooden. A small crevice lay ahead. Without a word of warning, Kyle stepped neatly over it. From behind came a sickening thump and a cry of pain. Cocking his head, Kyle turned toward Del, all the heaviness in his body suddenly gone.

6

Del

Del craned his head out the window of the bus as it climbed a logging road into the bleak, sun-parched foothills of the Sierras.

Mr. Dugan was trying to coax the campers into singing "Camptown Races." But everyone's eyes were riveted to the alien terrain: a daylit moonscape of rock cathedrals and avalanche-scarred ridgelines above them, and a vertiginous drop to the valley below. Sam Berkus, a counselor, drove the bus. He downshifted abruptly on a sharp turn, and Del instinctively gripped the armrest as though they would plunge headlong into the reeling emptiness at any second. Next to him, Gillian giggled. Del chuckled back nervously.

The bus rounded a tight, banked switchback and passed an abandoned ranger station. An orange snow-marker posted the altitude: five thousand feet. Del scratched fitfully at the thick dressing covering the cut on his cheek. He was lucky; he could have easily broken his leg falling into that crevice during capture the flag. Why hadn't Kyle told him to watch out? He snuck a quick glance back toward Kyle, who sat alone at the rear of the bus, dozing. Since Del's capture-the-flag accident, Kyle had been ignoring him.

"I want to learn how to start a fire by rubbing two sticks together," Page announced. "Sort of a scientific experiment."

"Sure thing, Professor," Miles said, rolling his eyes. "Beating your meat is about as close as *you'll* ever get."

"Speak for yourself, hotshot," Page countered. "It's just a question of finding the right type of wood. And a spindle and a bowstring and a lot of elbow grease. Think you can remember all that, or did I say it too fast?"

Del smiled to himself, secretly pleased to see Page holding his own against the older boy.

Mr. Dugan produced a shiny paperback from his pocket entitled *Wilderness Survival* "Try reading this instead of arguing," he suggested, opening the book. "You can use a camera. Just open up the back and let the sun focus through the lens on some wood shavings. You'll have your fire quicker than you can say Jack Sprat. What do *you* say, Gordie?"

"There are better ways." Gordon suddenly pulled a twelve-gauge shotgun shell from his pocket. "Kyle—think fast." He tossed it at the dozing boy.

The shell bounced off Kyle's chest, startling him awake. He looked up in confusion.

"Pick up the shell and pull the cap off," Gordon instructed. "What's inside?"

Kyle looked down at the contents and shook his head.

"Looks like shredded steel wool soaked in paint thinner, doesn't it?" Gordon continued. "What do you think it's for?"

"Starting a fire?" Del volunteered.

"You got it. Instant tinder. But even tinder won't help you unless that survival gear upstairs knows how to use it. Take another example: your water supply. Let's say your canteen is empty. What do you do?"

"I know," Del piped in.

Gordon ignored him. "Kyle?"

"I don't know. Find a 7-Eleven."

Del clucked his tongue in annoyance.

"Come on, Kyle, you can do better than that," Gordon insisted.

"Maybe find a stream somewhere?"

"And then what?"

"Go for it."

"That's exactly what you *don't* do. You never ever drink untreated water from a mountain stream."

"You mean there's even pollution up here?" Page said.

Gordon nodded. "You've got to boil the water first, or purify it with iodine tablets. Otherwise you might have *Giardia* to contend with."

"*Giardia*? Sounds like pasta," Miles said, affecting an Italian accent. "Fettuccine, mozzarella, pass the *Giardia*, mamma mia!" He elicited a few giggles and grins from the others. Gordon remained tight-lipped.

"Cute, Miles. But I wouldn't wish *Giardia* on anyone. It's the last word in gastrointestinal poisoning. You'd be so sick you couldn't even read the directions on the Maalox bottle."

The bus turned abruptly off the logging road into a lush meadow ringed by foxtail pines. At the far end of the clearing a foaming creek bubbled invitingly. There was no parking lot, no cars, or other hikers in sight. *We'll have The Wilds all to ourselves,* Del thought, pleased. He spotted a trail that zigzagged up the mountain and disappeared over a rise. Beyond it, three snowy minarets reared up into seamless blue sky from an amphitheater of green glacier ice.

"Let's shake a leg now, campers," Mr. Dugan said as Sam parked near the trailhead. "Everyone get your own rucksack from the back of the bus. If any of you girls need help, ask Gillian. She's volunteered to fill in for Cindy as much as she can. Think of her as your deputy counselor."

Deputy counselor? Del thought, surprised, glancing at her. "A promotion," he said, patting her leg. Gillian shrugged and smiled.

While the campers unloaded their gear, Sam helped Gordon loop two coils of Perlon mountaineering rope to his pack. Mr. Dugan had the older boys carry tents. Because of his size, Del hoisted the propane stove on his back.

"All right, are we ready?" Mr. Dugan asked, brandishing a stout oak walking stick. Everyone cheered and whistled. "We'll see you tomorrow night, Sam. Be there or be square!"

Sam chuckled and hopped back into the bus. "I'll bring you guys plenty of hot chocolate in Thermoses."

"Onward and upward, soldiers," Mr. Dugan shouted. "One foot in front of the other now."

"Watch out for snakes, everybody," Gordon warned. "There are rattlers up here."

In high spirits, the campers slung on their packs and followed the two counselors over the creek on a log bridge. Del heard the bus horn beep twice in farewell. Sam waved out the window as the bus lumbered away, disappearing into the trees.

A blazed footpath led the group uphill through a thick alcove of willow, then into arid foothills covered with chest-high chaparral and sagebrush. It was an easy climb at first, but the grade slowly steepened and the trail grew fainter, snaking between boulders the size of Volkswagens. Del and Gillian took the lead behind the counselors, Kyle a steady distance behind them. Page and Jennifer kept up, but the majority quickly fell back, stopping frequently to catch their breath. Lonny lagged far behind everyone. "Don't leave me, don't leave me!" he cried.

Del felt winded. His shoulder blades ached from the abrasion of the pack straps, and his feet chafed in his boots. But he refused to stop; he had to set an example. Kyle appeared to know something about carrying a pack. He walked with his back erect in a slow but smooth, unvarying gait.

"Come along, you chuckleheads!" Mr. Dugan shouted cheerily, clambering over a fallen sequoia.

"Fuck this shit," Miles muttered, wheezing.

"If you're at all serious about joining the Wolf Pack, Miles, you'd better improve that attitude," Mr. Dugan warned.

"Yeah, right."

The Wolf Pack, Del knew, was Wolf Gulch's answer to the Camper Hall of Fame. At the end of every summer, one exemplary junior woodsman would have his or her name inscribed on a mahogany plaque in the director's office. Del doubted the others could live up to its standards. Haines was too impulsive, always acting before thinking. Miles was a bully. Kyle might make a potential woodsman, but he wasn't a participator. Little Lonny was a walking disaster. Ironically, younger campers like Page and Jennifer seemed to be faring better than the older kids. But small fry never won the Wolf Pack award. Del hoped the honor would be his.

After an hour on the trail, the group reached a small plateau. The land here was devoid of vegetation, except for a pair of stunted foxtail pines clinging grimly to the striated granite.

The gnarled, desiccated trees looked more like rock than wood. A redwood sign was bolted to a snow marker on a bare stub of stone:

"THE WILDS"
NATIONAL WILDERNESS AREA
Dangerous Terrain
Follow Red Tags
PLEASE HELP PREVENT FOREST FIRES

Majestic corrugated ridges, each successively higher, encircled the hikers with frightening scale. There was no sign of either man or civilization, only the utter stillness of nature.

Mr. Dugan called a rest stop.

"Want to play King of the Mountain, Del?" Jennifer tasked, leaping atop a ledge like a young mountain goat.

Short of breath, Del shook his head and sat heavily on a lichen-spotted boulder. He tried to swallow a handful of trail mix, but could barely get it down. His stomach was a knot, his throat too constricted to accept even water from his canteen. He felt dizzy and nauseous. *Must be altitude sickness*, he thought, ashamed of himself. He couldn't let the others see his condition.

"Yikes, what's that?" Lonny yelped in horror, pointing at something.

Del leaned over and saw a blackened animal skull, half buried in rotted duff.

"Hmmm," Mr. Dugan said, picking it up gingerly. "What have we here?"

Del peered closer, then gasped. For a split second, he had thought the eyehole of the skull had glanced directly at him.

Something papery and black floated to the ground like a grotesque leaf. It was a flap of withered flesh. Most everyone stepped back, repulsed.

"Looks like a bear skull," Gordon said.

"What killed it?" Page asked, intrigued.

"Mother Nature has her ways, son," Mr. Dugan said. "All right now," he called out. "Let's get the train back on the tracks here." He heaved the skull into the bushes.

"Don't leave me behind!" Lonny whimpered.

"You're such a *whiner*, Lonny," Jennifer said. "I'm sick of listening to you." She produced a pack of Garbage Pail Kids playing cards from her pocket and shuffled through a disgusting assortment of barters, nose-pickers, and pant-shitters. "Here, this is for you, Lonny." She handed him *Nailed Noel*, a boy hanging from a wall by a nail driven through his tongue. "This is what happens to whiners when they don't shut up."

"Come along now," Mr. Dugan shouted. "Last one up has to dig the latrine tonight."

Del dragged himself to his feet. As soon as they were moving again, the nausea abated. But he still felt lightheaded.

Gordon pointed to the west. "Look yonder. See that little pass between the pinnacles? That's Skyline Fireroad. That's where Sam will pick us up tomorrow night."

"Seems pretty close to me," Page remarked, tugging absently on his cowlick.

"It may look close, but that's a good twenty miles as the crow flies." Gordon turned to address the others. "Don't forget what I told you: It's easy to lose your way around here. Make *sure* you follow the blazes—those red tags. And *don't* stray off under any circumstances."

"You mean we can't do any exploring?" Del asked with some disappointment, inspecting the blisters on his rock-bruised heels.

"Absolutely not. Those little side trails may look tempting but they go nowhere. It's easy to get lost and confused."

"We could leave a trail of something," Jennifer offered.

"Bread crumbs," Lissa suggested. "Like Hansel and Gretel."

"Birds eat bread crumbs, dummy," Page pointed out.

"And remember, Lissa, Hansel and Gretel almost didn't make it out alive," Gordon said with measured heaviness.

"Jeez, man," Del mumbled. "Lighten up."

"Excuse me?"

"Nothing. Forget it."

"What did you say, Del?" Gordon insisted. "Come on, spit it out."

Del furrowed his brow. "I just don't think you should keep scaring the little guys like that."

"You still don't get it, do you? I *want* to scare them. For their own good."

"Honestly, Gordon," Mr. Dugan warned.

"Kids, all I'm saying is that The Wilds is a tricky place," said Gordon. "It's a labyrinth." He hesitated. "It's almost like these mountains *want* you to get lost. Do you buy that, Del?"

Del shrugged and moved on, tension in his walk.

Gordon sidled over to him as they labored uphill. "At this point, I really expect a little more cooperation from you, Del. You've got a good sense of leadership, so use it. Help me keep these kids in line—okay?" He smiled.

Del nodded, relaxing a little. "Okay."

The trail traversed a sunny draw and led the group deep into a primeval forest. The treetops entwined overhead in a lofty canopy, shutting out sunlight to evoke a lush, shadowy world. Century-old fir and ponderosa sighed and swayed in the breeze, redolent with the warm smells of mildew, fungus, and pine. Poison oak and white mushrooms flourished on the sun-dappled forest floor.

The group stopped for an early lunch in a clearing bordered by wild laurel and dotted with showy clumps of mustang clover. The main course was Spam sandwiches. Del took one look at the pinkish meat and grimaced. His stomach did a flip.

"I just can't eat this," he confided quietly to Mr. Dugan.

"Got to keep up your strength, son," Dugan replied. "It's going to be a long hike."

"Right, sir."

When the camp director turned away, Del pitched his lunch into the bushes. Noticing this, Lewis scrambled to retrieve the sandwich.

"What are you doing?" Del whispered. "Leave it alone."

"I'm still hungry," Lewis said.

Jennifer promptly handed him one of her Garbage Pail Kids cards: *Seymour Barf*, a boy regurgitating violently. "Don't be such a pig," she warned, "or that'll be you."

The others gobbled down their lunch, some letting their sandwich wrappings blow across the meadow. Del knitted his eyebrows in consternation.

Somebody ought to take charge here. Somebody ought to make them clean up this mess.

He bridled under all of Gordon's stringent rules and precautions. The man was such a maniac about safety—and yet he let everyone litter. He was a hypocrite!

A pair of gray squirrels scaled a tree above the campers, stalking a bird's nest. The mother bird, a mountain chickadee, according to Gordon, flitted in nervous circles overhead and chirped piteously. Miles and Haines began pelting the squirrels with an arsenal of empty soda cans.

"Hey, you two, cut that out!" Gillian shouted, moving in to confiscate the remaining ammunition.

"What do you think you're doing?" Haines protested.

"I can do anything I want," she retorted. "I'm the deputy counselor."

"Then suck wind, counselor," Miles said.

Del intervened. "Cut it out, guys. And pick up those cans."

"Who does she think she is?" Miles grumbled.

Gillian looked him dead in the eye. "How would *you* like it if someone took a shot at you?"

"It's just some stupid squirrels," Miles said.

"The hell it is. Animals have rights too."

"Gillian's got a point there," Mr. Dugan said. "I didn't know you were such an animal-libber. The Sierra Club's very big on that sort of thing, I suppose."

Gillian nodded. "I think it's important."

"What a bunch of bogus B.S.," Miles complained. "We were stopping the squirrels from eating the eggs. Why should a squirrel's life be worth more than a baby bird's life?"

"Survival of the fittest, Miles," Mr. Dugan said, directing his words toward Kyle. "In nature or civilization, it's always the same: Life is war."

Kyle didn't seem to be listening, Del noticed. He wondered if Kyle cared a hoot about survival, let alone the conversation.

After the meal, the campers lazed back in the tall grass for a brief siesta. Gordon passed around the invaluable topographic map he carried in his breast pocket, labeled U.S. GEOLOGICAL SURVEY, SERIES II, BEAR CLAW QUADRANT. Del tried to find their position, but the map was indecipherable, a myriad of wavy, concentric lines winding across splotches of blue and green.

"It's so quiet up here," Kyle remarked.

Gordon nodded. "The writer Jack London once called it the 'White Silence.'" He faced the rest of the campers. "Let's try a little experiment here. I want everyone to be absolutely still. Just listen to the White Silence. All of you now, close your eyes and breathe deep. Allow your minds to clear. Be alert to anything you usually *don't* hear."

Everyone fell silent. Del listened intently but could not keep his eyes shut for more than a few seconds. Even as he tried to tune in to the whispering wind, his mind swarmed with distractions. He could only hear the rhythmic tattoo of his own heartbeat. Then slowly, imperceptibly at first, he became aware of an almost subliminal vibration *beyond* the silence: a long low-decibel note, an aural mirage. The hypnagogic hum surrounded him with an eerie, tangible presence that seemed to extend beyond the clearing, encompassing all of The Wilds.

Glip-glip

He heard the incongruous sound of bubbling water.

Glip ... glip

The sound had a magical, alluring ring to it, a melodic riff played on crystal. Del opened his eyes.

Glip-glip-glip

The string of shimmering notes danced on the wind, a bubbling refrain sounding ever louder, closer, beckoning irresistibly. What was it, a brook? Why hadn't the others heard it? They were still in their meditative repose, eyes closed. The lilting phrase *glipped* again and again in Del's mind like wind chimes.

Del rose to his feet and crept silently to the edge of the forest. He peered into the wooded darkness. For a moment, he thought he saw a quick, faraway flash of silver, sunlight reflecting off a rushing mountain brook.

With a quick glance over his shoulder, he slipped into the woods. He came upon a tiny path and followed it, twisting and turning through thick stands of lodgepole pine and sugar maple. There were deer prints and bear droppings. The moss felt velvet-soft underfoot. Sunlight filtered down through the treetop canopy in bold, ethereal shafts. Mica flecks glittered in the rocks.

There's something incredibly alive about this place.

It was like an enchanted forest, a magical storybook world.

Del soon realized that the brook was farther away than he had first reckoned. The trail split, then split again. Del faltered. Should he go on? Gordon had warned about these labyrinthine side paths, and Del had broken the rules. Gordon would burn his ass for sure. And yet Del could not turn back; these ancient trees seemed so old and wise, so fascinating. They knew more about life and death than he could ever imagine. His life's priorities—high grades for college, campaigning for president of his class, pleasing his parents—no longer possessed any more substance than a dream.

Something wonderful is going to happen.

He sensed it without a flicker of doubt: A great truth was about to be unveiled. This eldritch forest knew secrets about *him*, Del Albright. But what did it know? He had to find out.

The foliage grew denser as Del advanced, more tangled and forbidding. The shadows deepened oppressively. He could smell the ozone, taste the moisture in the air. Del felt like an explorer, a pioneer, perhaps the first human being ever to tread this path.

But what else had walked here before him?

The trail rose into a new sector of woods recently ravaged by a forest fire. The ruined landscape made Del uneasy. Spiky, denuded firs and dead-black snags groped skyward. In the inhuman light, the twisted roots of a fallen aspen jutted out like the talons of a gnarled claw. Burnt branches tore at Del, streaking his parka with black, ugly smudges.

Fires are good for the forest, Del thought, trying to calm his nerves. *They renew the cycle of life.*

The path shrank until Del had to place one foot before the other, as carefully as a tightrope walker. *Where is that brook?* he wondered dimly, pushing onward. His brain did not seem to be functioning quite right. The water had to be just ahead. He could faintly make out its lovely murmurings, high and low notes, snatches of a voice he yearned to hear clearly.

Hard ground gave way to brackish, oozing mud. *Got to mark my way,* he told himself, stopping to post a fallen branch in the soft earth. He recalled Lissa's bread crumbs and tried to smile.

Farther on, the sound of running water grew louder, metamorphosing into the ominous rumble of a colossal waterfall. But to his frustration, Del could still see no sign of it beyond the mesh of brush and bramble.

This is impossible.

He tripped over something that writhed and caught hold of his leg. Del recoiled with a gasp. It was only a creeper, but it had tightened around his ankle like a boa constrictor. Agitated, he tore it loose and was about to take a step forward when he saw blue sky through the brambles at his feet.

Del was standing at the edge of a sheer, camouflaged precipice. Shaken, he scrambled away and retraced his steps to the last fork in the path.

He stopped to catch his breath, giddy and disoriented. The taunting sound of rushing water came from all sides now. Sweat broke out on the back of his neck. He'd never find that brook—maybe there never was a brook. The Wilds had tricked him. Could he find his way back to the clearing?

Then the smell hit him: a thick, cloying rot-stink that filled his lungs, threatening to coalesce into something too horrible to conceive. Del staggered into a spider web that wrapped around his face like a death veil. He frantically brushed it away.

Reaching the fork, he groped for the marking stick he had left behind. It was gone, the earth where he had planted it now smooth. Was this the right fork? The sound of rushing water grew still louder; it brayed like a wind organ holding onto a shrieking lunatic chord.

A twig snapped close behind him.

Del stiffened to a halt with the eerie, intuitive feeling that something was moving through the brush on the other side of the foliage, something was tracking him. Was it a bear? A mountain lion? His thoughts went careening in all directions. It was the Donner Man, Gordon's hulking German cannibal, stalking him with red, glittering eyes and dripping jaws. Del had disobeyed Gordon and trespassed into the Donner Man's dominion. The predator could smell his fear and was biding its time, waiting for the right moment to burst through and devour him in a flesh-hungry frenzy.

Del thought he heard a low, short growl from behind the foliage. He turned away, trembling, the hair at the back of his neck bristling. Perhaps it was just a tree limb moaning in the wind. Then the growl ran up the scale to a plangent screech that shook the whole of his body. Del realized with detached fuzziness that it was the sound of his own piercing scream.

Another twig snapped behind him. Del sprinted ahead in a blind, pounding run. He heard the Donner Man come after him with heavy, loping footfalls. It was panting and bleating in the thrill of the chase. He couldn't, mustn't, look back. Pure fight-or-flight instinct guided him back through the weaving labyrinth, leading him on a route only his subconscious knew.

A hundred yards ahead, a rainbow blaze of light beamed out like a searchlight—the clearing. Adrenaline electrified Del's muscles, and he ran faster than he ever had in his life. With a wail of anguish, he tore into the sunny meadow and fell to his knees, sobbing, his jeans puckering wet across his groin.

7

Kyle

Kyle grimaced when the mountain path led the group above the canopy of the forest. He pulled down the brim of his leather cap and squinted into the harsh sunlight of the rocky, denuded Sierra face.

Without the camouflage of conifers, it would be difficult, if not impossible, to avoid Del. Kyle was responsible for Del's fall during capture the flag; it had been a flash of anger, an impulse. But Kyle owed Del for that, and he couldn't face him. So he deliberately lagged behind the group, pretending he was on his own private hike.

"Come along, Kyle," Mr. Dugan called back to him. "We don't want any dawdlers here."

"I'm not dawdling. I'm just taking in the scenery."

"Let's go now, soldier, one foot in front of the other."

Soldier? Kyle snorted to himself. What was this, boot camp?

"We're coming up to a promontory called the Dragonback," Gordon announced. "It's going to be a hard climb from here on."

The headwall rose before them like some huge pagan idol. The sight of it made Kyle almost queasy with awe. Rockslide paths and fans of shale rubble scored its flanks. Stone buttes of iron ore, stained red by mineral seeps, jutted out of the scree—the dragon's fangs. Harsh wind blew down in a foul weather warning: *Stay away.*

Trudging around the next switchback, Kyle was surprised to find Gordon backtracking down the trail. "You seen my canteen, Kyle? I think I left it down at that spring."

Kyle shook his head.

"You doing okay?"

Kyle shrugged. "Sure."

"By the way, you didn't have anything to do with stealing the camp bus last night, did you?"

"No."

"I hope you're telling the truth," Gordon said softly, scrutinizing him. "I'd be awfully disappointed if you weren't. I think a lot of you, Kyle."

The bones in Kyle's neck cracked. "I said I didn't do it. You sound like someone's father or something."

"I just asked."

"You're *not* my dad."

"Okay, okay." Gordon chuckled. "I definitely don't want to be that. God knows my dad put *me* through enough hoops. I'd never want to do that to any son of mine."

Kyle eased off and almost smiled. "Don't worry, you'd make a lot better dad than mine."

Gordon brightened and clapped him on the back "I'll take that as a compliment."

The sound of falling stones overhead made them look up. A large antlered buck stood on a rock shelf just above them.

Kyle opened his mouth to say something, but Gordon touched his shoulder. The buck pawed the earth and studied them with probing eyes. Kyle did not look away. The animal's ears fluttered in tiny arcs, its nostrils flaring. As if backing away from a challenge, the deer bowed his magnificent five-point crown of antlers.

For a moment, neither Kyle nor Gordon could speak. Kyle thought he saw tears in Gordon's eyes. Gordon nodded silently, as if reading his mind.

A shout from uphill shattered the moment: "Hey, what's going on?" Del came marching down the trail.

Startled, the buck darted quickly out of sight.

"What happened to you guys?" Del said. "Mr. Dugan sent me down to find you."

Gordon blew his nose. "We were looking for my canteen. Guess it's still down at that creek."

"I'll go for it," Kyle volunteered, hoping to avoid Del.

Gordon shook his head. "No way. Nobody else goes off alone on this trek." He flashed a dark glance at Del. After lunch, Del had mysteriously vanished. Gordon had gotten unbelievably angry at his disappearance and had been organizing a search party when Del had come bursting out of the forest as if the devil were on his tail.

"Why don't I go down with Kyle?" Del suggested. "You know, the buddy system. Two can survive better than one. Like the Wolf Pack."

Say no, say no, Kyle prayed.

Gordon thought for a moment, then nodded. "I suppose that's all right. Just don't waste any time down there. And if you don't find the canteen right away, start back up without it. We'll wait for you up top."

"Yes sir," Del replied like a good soldier, watching Gordon head uphill. "Boy is he in an awful mood today," he added in a low voice.

With a sigh, Kyle doffed his pack and started downhill.

"Some trek, huh?" Del said, matching his stride.

"Not too shabby." An awkward silence ensued. "What happened to you after lunch, anyway?" Kyle said finally. Gordon had given Del a severe tongue-lashing for disobeying the rules of the hike and going off on his own.

"Thought I heard a mountain stream nearby," Del said in a thin voice.

Kyle angrily kicked a pinecone over the cliff and watched it plummet to the forest below. "Look," he began haltingly, "about last night—"

"We shouldn't have taken that damn arroyo," Del broke in. "I don't blame you for being pissed about it."

Kyle blanched in surprise. "*Me* pissed?"

"Guess it was my own stupid fault."

Del was genuinely upset, Kyle realized in amazement. He wasn't blaming Kyle for what happened. Trusting their friendship, Del still believed it had been an accident! One "blood brother" would never deliberately try and hurt another, would he?

Feeling small and despicable, and at the same time angry, Kyle increased his stride, trying not to let Del catch up.

"Hey," Del called out. Kyle didn't stop. "What is this, a footrace?"

Kyle half-turned, irritated. "I'd just as soon be by myself right now."

Del looked at him askance, his brow wrinkling.

"Why don't you go catch up with the others. I'll be right back."

"Sure," Del said with an injured look. "Catch you later."

Kyle heard the receding crunch of Del's footsteps, but would not look back.

8

Gordon

Gordon hastened up the trail toward the main group. The elation of the wondrous moment shared with Kyle and the buck faded as new worries set in. Maybe it hadn't been such a good idea letting Del and Kyle go down the trail by themselves. You could never let your guard down in The Wilds. He could trust Kyle, but Del was more likely to go off half-cocked again, do something rash.

The incline steepened and Gordon's breath came in short rasps. He decided that tonight, after they made camp at Lost Lake, he would offer to give mountain-climbing lessons to the older boys. Kyle would be the best candidate. Gordon would demonstrate the basics, show Kyle that not all dads were fools and jackasses.

Scanning the Sierra rim, Gordon noticed the white contrail of a military jet. He thought it might be an old T-38 Talon, and wondered nostalgically if it was one of the restored birds he had worked on in Palmdale.

After the Billy Robin incident, Gordon had cashed his final paycheck, packed a suitcase, and left Milwaukee, driving west without destination. He had four months to decide if he would accept Wolf Gulch's standing offer for another summer in The Wilds. In the meantime, he felt like a bum, a drifter. At the age of twenty-seven, he had accomplished nothing. The days blurred together: hypnotic ribbons of freeway; greasy, depressing meals in truck stops; suspicious night clerks in low-rent motels.

A week later, Gordon found himself in the Mojave Desert near Palmdale, California. Off the highway, he noticed a menagerie of exotic military jets parked on a scrubby, rundown airstrip. There were T-38 Talons, Lockheed T-33s, even an A-4 Skyhawk like the ones he had worked on in wartime Saigon. What were they doing on a private field? he wondered. The Air Force doesn't sell off its used supersonic stock; nearly all mothballed military jets are stripped and flattened by bulldozers. Intrigued, Gordon turned off to check it out.

Within the hour he had landed himself a job as a restoration mechanic at Howard DeRosa Air Restoration. The company specialized in rebuilding the rare demilitarized warbirds for fat-cat flying enthusiasts willing to pay the price for a supersonic toy. The T-38 Talon had come off an airport pillar in Cody, Wyoming, where it had hung like a moosehead trophy ever since the Tet Offensive.

The next day Gordon fell quickly into the work, sorting out skeins of colored wires in the open fuselage of the reconstructed Skyhawk. It was an easy, mindless job, and he enjoyed the solitude of the desert. Sometimes he would spend an entire shift without speaking to anyone. He liked the feel of the sun beating down on his bare back, the rhythmic tick of the galvanized hangar roof shuddering in the hot breeze. He liked the rebuilding and testing, the control, the satisfaction of squeezing out every last ounce of performance. Gone were the Pop Holloses and Billy Robins of life, that terrible feeling of impotence. He stopped thinking about the manuscript pages tucked away on top of the Frigidaire in his rented cottage; they slowly disappeared under an accumulation of forwarded, unopened envelopes from Milwaukee.

Gordon knew now that his old psych prof had been dead on target: He *was* a dream chaser. He just didn't have the dedication or drive to push beyond his own limitations and prove everyone wrong. The book itself seemed to him now like a lucid dream— an unreality of his own making.

In Palmdale, Gordon had at last found peace of mind. He liked the Tex-Mex food and tequila at the local watering holes, the flying stories swapped with space shuttle techies and Air Force fly-boys. But most of all, he liked his boss and drinking buddy, Howard DeRosa.

Here was a man utterly content with his life. Howard knew how to live one day at a time, enjoying the *now*. He never tortured himself about what might have been or what could happen tomorrow—so different from Gordon, who relentlessly picked the scabs off his old emotional wounds. Gordon came to view the older man as a kind of surrogate father. Howard helped him see himself clearly for the first time. He made Gordon realize it was time to jump off that freight train that had rumbled destructively through his life.

"*Hey, you can't* help *being a washout*," Dad had hammered home. "*Being an iggerant runs in the family.*"

Blowing it all, washing out in the Hollos tradition, had always been safer than finishing anything. Without realizing it, Gordon had kept an unspoken pact with old Pop Hollos: to keep failing. Like father, like son. Success would have threatened the bond between them, and Gordon couldn't risk abandonment by his only kin. But even now, with Dad dead and gone, Gordon still needed his approval; he was still trapped in childhood.

Then he discovered mountain climbing. Howard introduced him to the sport, starting him out on basic rock work in the nearby San Gabriel Mountains.

"*Climbing brings you down to basics*," Howard told him. "*It's therapeutic. A mountain always makes you pay for your screw-ups.*"

The first time Howard challenged him to try rappelling, Gordon balked. He couldn't believe the thin, stretchy rope would actually support his weight. The act of stepping backward off the edge of a cliff was frightening and absolutely insane—it went against all instinct.

Once he took that first step, however, the rest was easy. To his surprise, Gordon was in complete control, pushing joyfully off the cliff face in bigger and bigger leaps, the rope playing out through the carabiner on his harness. Something about Gordon's body and the mountain face seemed to click; they understood one another. He had never felt more alive. Teaching driver's ed, he had felt much closer to death.

Gordon became a mountaineering enthusiast, he couldn't get enough of it. He spent every weekend honing his skills in the Tehachapis, the San Jacintos, the Santa Ynez. During the week, he pored over survival manuals, mountaineering textbooks, and glossy climbing magazines. Howard told him he was a natural, a quick learner. Gordon was amazed—he had never been a natural at anything. Climbing required total concentration. When he was clinging to chinks in a vertical face, there was no place for that critical voice in his head; he had only the mountain to judge him. At last he had found a vocation with real challenge and fulfillment. Never mind the wasted years, the useless psychology studies, the unwritten book. He would become a professional climber, a mountain guide.

One night over tequila and Dos Equis chasers, Gordon unloaded the whole story on Howard—the Wolf Gulch Ordeal and Cal Wolcroft's death. Gordon still hadn't decided whether to accept the standing job offer.

"You owe it to yourself to go back to those mountains," Howard had advised. *"If I had to live with what you went through, I'd always be asking myself how I would perform given a second chance, I'd have to put myself through the same ordeal, just to see how I'd do. To face my demons down, get free of them. That's what mountain climbing is all about!"*

Then and there, Gordon had decided he would go back for a final season at Wolf Gulch. This time he would be prepared, he would know how to handle The Wilds. No mountain would ever mess with him again.

9

Kyle

Kyle fairly skipped down the trail to retrieve Gordon's canteen. Just being alone was a relief. He was free of Del now, free of worry. A mountain breeze softly caressed his hair, revitalizing him. Slowing his gait, Kyle observed vividly colored alpine wildflowers he had not seen during the ascent: shooting star, buttercup, Indian paintbrush. Overhead, a pair of hawks played tag with the wind currents. This was what he had wanted—*his* Wilds.

To his disappointment, Kyle quickly found the canteen half-hidden in the reeds lining the creek. Now he would have to rejoin the others, face Del again. He knelt down and dunked his head in a deep aquamarine pool of spring water. The icy chill made him draw back, and he shook himself like a spaniel.

On impulse, Kyle doffed his clothes and dove into the pool with almost reckless abandon. The shock of the water stunned him; his scrotum tightened. Exhilarated, he kicked down into the depths and bumped along the green bottom, silky algae tickling his belly, hands poised at his sides like fins.

Gliding back toward the surface, he exhaled. A burst of silvery bubbles roared past his ears *from a purple, screaming mouth. The hands clawed up at him. The bulging eyes pleaded for mercy.*

Kyle gagged and breathed in a lungful of water.

Firm hands held him down. He could not break away.

He hurtled to the surface in a frenzy of flailing arms and legs. Gasping for breath, he splashed crazily to shore and crawled out on all fours, collapsing on a sun-warmed slab, chest heaving.

"Kyle! Where is your brother, young man?"

Sobbing, Kyle curled into a fetal ball. He dug his fingernails into his palms until he drew blood.

Blood brothers.

Kyle squeezed his eyes shut. A familiar face swam into the blackness behind his eyelids—a face he knew too well.

Go away!

But Marshall grinned at him fondly with his lopsided, all-knowing smile.

Marshall had powers; only Kyle knew of them. Marshall wasn't as crazy as everyone said—his five senses were just more developed. Marshall had eyes like a cat; he could see shadows in a pitch-black room. His hearing was so acute he could detect the filament burning in a fight bulb. To Marshall, the odor of human sweat was a rotting stench, impossible to bear.

"Jesus, Kyle! I thought you were watching him!"

Marshall was autistic. The sensory pathways to his brain were like ten-lane superhighways, barraging him with an overload of information. He could not tolerate it, he had closed himself off to survive. Human touch repelled him. The only sensations that pleased him were the ones he inflicted upon himself.

"Stop it, Marshall! Holy shit, what have you done to your arm?"

Marshall was gnawing at his wrist. Then he began methodically smacking his forehead against the sharp edge of the table. Blood streaked his face. His mouth frothed. Kyle grabbed him, but Marshall writhed out of his arms like a monster fish.

"Dad's going to freak out again, you know that. I know *you know that, man!"*

Spittle dribbled from the corner of Marshall's mouth. With a quivering shriek, he wrenched free and twirled in a spinning circle until he collapsed in a puddle of vomit. Then he riveted Kyle with that mystic, intimidating half-smile, as if Marshall could see into his soul.

"KYLE! WHAT THE HELL HAVE YOU DONE TO THIS CHILD?"

Life was an unending torment for Marshall, a nightmare he could never escape. He was trapped in the prison of his own short-circuited senses. Smearing himself with his own feces broke an instinctive rule of the animal kingdom shared by every living creature. But it gave the world a smell Marshall could tolerate, an odor he could control at will. It was the only way he could survive. No human being deserved that kind of existence, Kyle had finally realized. That was why he had put an end to it, freed Marshall from his torment.

They had done it together.

They were accomplices together, even though Marshall fought back at the end, his face swelling and turning purple as he drowned in the bathtub. Fighting off compassion, Kyle held him under until it was over. It was an act of love.

Kyle sat up with a jerk. What time was it? The sun had inched much closer to the mountain horizon. The others would be waiting at the summit, wondering where he was. If he didn't arrive soon, Gordon would send someone down after him— maybe Del. Kyle's stomach tightened; he quickly dressed and laced up his hiking boots. He wished he could stay on here, sleep under the stars on a bed of pine boughs, alone. Or maybe with Gordon. They were both loners like that buck. Together they could have explored The Wilds in all its wonder. There would be no demands, no expectations to live up to.

Begrudgingly, Kyle started back up the steep switchbacks. It seemed to take forever to reach the place where he had left Del. Further on, Kyle paused at the spot where the buck had confronted him and Gordon. He hoisted his backpack on and moved ahead. The added weight further slowed his uphill progress.

Strings of breath-sapping switchbacks looped and relooped endlessly onto themselves. Kyle came to an unmarked fork. One path led steeply upward; the other, more trodden, continued in a mild traverse. Where was the red tag to point the way? He would have to make a choice. Common sense led him to take the more beaten path. But after a hundred yards, there was still no sign of a tag. Kyle squinted into the sun, trying to reconnoiter across the mocking expanse of broken rock. His pulse quickened. What if he were caught on the Dragonback overnight?

"Hey guys!" he hollered uphill. "Where are you?"

Needles of fear prickled the base of his spine. He hastened on.

The path narrowed and crossed a sheer cliff face. Kyle clambered over a withered, sun-whitened tree trunk that had fallen across the path. Ahead he saw that the trail was washed out—impassable. He turned back angrily. It had been the wrong trail after all.

The tree trunk suddenly cracked and gave way underfoot. Kyle lost his balance and fell with it over the side of the cliff.

He lunged instinctively, catching hold of a spindly bush while the trunk bounced noisily down the Dragonback. All he could do was wrap his arms around the protruding roots of the bush and dangle, spiderlike, not daring to look down. His toes dug desperately into the cliff face. His hands began to cramp and his arms broke out in gooseflesh.

I won't look down. I can't look down.

But he had to. It was not the sheer, vertical drop he had expected, but a steep, serrated granite incline.

The wind picked up—a fierce current of living air that wanted to suck him off the mountain.

10

Del

From the bald craggy summit, Del scoured the cliffs below for a sign of Kyle. He was perched atop a Jeffrey pine that angled vertiginously out over the precipice. As if challenging the sheer drop beneath him, Del tore off a strip of bark and hurled it over the edge. It twisted and turned, bouncing off the rock outcrops as a body might tumble from great heights.

"Del! Get down from there immediately," Mr. Dugan ordered.

Del did not comply.

Gordon scanned the Dragonback, shaking his head with slow-burning agitation. "This never should have happened. Goddamnit, Del, it was *your* responsibility to stay with him!"

"But I told you, he made me—"

"I don't want to hear any excuses. That was your last screw-up, buddy. Any more and we're all going back down to the Gulch. *Comprende?* Now go get me my climbing gear."

"Yes sir," Del said, lowering his head contritely. He jumped down from his tree perch and trudged uphill to a cairn where the backpacks had been left, away from the others.

"I can't understand it," Mr. Dugan said, puzzled. "The path was clearly marked."

"It's this *place*, Jerry."

"There!" Gillian shouted from a rocky pinnacle, pointing. "I see him."

Mr. Dugan focused his binoculars down the face. "Good Lord, he's stuck down there on the mountainside."

They all leaned over the precipice for a look.

"How the hell …" Gordon murmured.

"There was a fork in the path," Page reasoned. "He must have taken the wrong trail."

"Maybe there wasn't a tag," Gillian said.

"Of course there was a tag," Gordon said. He quickly uncoiled his climbing rope. "I'm going down for him." He turned to Del who had come back with the gear. "Del, help me with this."

Del held a steel climbing clip while Gordon looped the rope around a large fissured boulder and secured it with a series of complicated knots.

"Can I help?" Jennifer asked.

"No. Del, help me keep everybody clear," Gordon said.

Del quickly hustled Jennifer and the others away from the edge. They looked dazed; things were happening too quickly. Even Mr. Dugan was at a loss for what to do.

"I'll rappel down and secure him," Gordon said, addressing everyone. "Then you guys haul us back, *slowly*, one at a time. Now let's test the rope."

"Come on, everyone," Mr. Dugan said, taking over. He and six campers tugged and jerked the line. The boulder held fast.

At the cliff edge, Gordon straddled the rope and brought it around his left hip, across his chest, over the right shoulder and down across his back.

"All set." With a quick thumbs-up gesture, he jumped backward over the lip of the summit, using his left hand to control the payout of the rope.

Moving to the edge, Del watched him rappel down the precipice, flying in great leaps away from the cliff face as though magically freed from gravity.

11

Gordon

A biting upwind made Gordon's descent harder than expected. He had to slow his downward momentum to keep from fouling his lines. Kyle looked to be in a bad way, and Gordon wasn't sure he could reach him in time.

What the devil had happened to that red tag?

Buffeted sideways by the wind, Gordon braked himself to a stop ten feet above Kyle's head. The boy looked up at him, grimacing with fear.

"You okay?"

Kyle managed to nod. He was clinging to a scrap of sagebrush.

"Hang in there. I'm coming down to tie you in from behind." He eased down the last ten feet until he was level with Kyle. "Now don't move."

"I *can't* move," Kyle gasped.

Wedging his heels in a fissure, Gordon made a weight shift and squatted over Kyle's back, straddling him.

The flap of the side pocket in Gordon's parka flew open in a gust of wind. A small bit of red plastic soared into space. Dumbfounded, Gordon stared at the tag until it disappeared from view. Fortunately, Kyle hadn't seen it.

A rush of adrenaline made Gordon dizzy as he prepared to secure Kyle with a bowline knot. Kyle's hand slipped and Gordon grabbed the boy by the sleeve. The weight threw Gordon off balance, slamming his braking hand against the rock wall. The rope came away from his fingers, and the two plunged downward, Kyle holding on to Gordon's leg for dear life.

12

Del

Gordon's hands clutched wildly, and he managed to break the uncontrolled rappel. He deposited Kyle and himself on a narrow ledge.

"They're safe!" Del tried to shout, but the words came out in a cracked whisper. He felt as if all the breath had been knocked out of him.

Gordon secured Kyle to the rope and signaled to Mr. Dugan for them to begin pulling.

Mr. Dugan mopped his brow on his sleeve. "All right now, I want Del, Haines, and Miles on the rope behind me."

"Let's have some teamwork here!" Del sang out as they raced to their positions. "Pull slowly, you guys. Dig in those toes for traction."

Mr. Dugan made a signal over the lip of the cliff and the boys began hoisting. Kyle was almost intolerably heavy. The rope jumped and writhed in Del's grasp, scraping away twists of skin, and he almost lost his grip.

Kyle's head finally appeared over the rock lip. He was in shock, his face the color of chalk.

"Easy now." Mr. Dugan grabbed Kyle's arms and lifted him the last few feet. The others broke out in relieved cheers.

"What happened?" Del asked, breathless.

"I don't know ..." Kyle's voice was dull and flat.

"Wrong fork."

"Didn't you see the red tag?" Miles demanded.

"There was no red tag."

"My ass there wasn't!"

"Stow it, son." Mr. Dugan tossed the rope back down to Gordon.

Kyle started to tremble violently. "There *was* no red tag, there *was* no red tag," he repeated urgently, staggering forward to lend a hand.

"No need for that," Mr. Dugan said, gently easing him aside.

"I'm okay," Kyle insisted, moving to join them.

Gordon had just put his weight on the rope when something whined behind them—an animal whimper. *That thing in the woods?* Del wondered for a panicked second.

It was the anchor boulder, moaning and creaking from the strain. It shifted, and a vibration—a *twang*—shuddered through Del's fingers. The rope slipped and came away with a horrible crack, whipsawing through the campers' flailing hands.

Mr. Dugan bellowed and grunted, struggling for control of the flying payout. Del felt the rope shredding the flesh from his fingers. He squeezed tighter. But no one could stop its awful momentum.

"Get away from the rope!" Mr. Dugan shrieked. The tendons on his neck jutted out in horrible relief. The rope, slick with blood, was nearly paid out. "I said, *GET AWAY FROM THE ROPE!*"

No one let go, but the rope zipped out of their grips. Screaming, Mr. Dugan turned his fists into a mangled brake, blood dripping over the rocks.

"*No!*" Del shouted, breaking into a run just as Mr. Dugan flew over the lip of the precipice. The camp director's piercing scream roiled up, a mounting caterwaul that echoed off the canyon walls.

The end of the rope shot over the ledge. The campers were alone.

13

Kyle

Kyle stared down the Dragonback, stunned. One body hung lifeless in the forest canopy; the other had disappeared. He focused groggily on his burned fingers, the blood oozing from the rope burns on his palms. The pain hadn't hit him yet.

Del stood rooted to the precipice. He was gazing into space with the glassy-eyed, dazed look of a child just awakened from a nightmare. Gillian cried quietly beside him, then turned away. Jennifer mumbled incoherently to herself, pacing in nervous circles. The others edged away from the cliff edge as if in slow motion. No one could speak. To Kyle, it seemed all too unreal.

The wind gathered strength, an icy downdraft tugging at Kyle's parka, beckoning him to follow Gordon and Mr. Dugan.

Come on now, one foot in front of the other, soldier.

Taking those few steps would be easier than what lay ahead of them, Kyle knew.

"Wow!" Miles broke the silence, turning to Del. "I don't fucking believe it! Did you see the way he just *bounced* off the rocks?"

"Shut up." Del fought back an attack of dry heaves. He slumped back against the anchor boulder, rubbing his eyes with his lacerated fingers, the blood blotching his face.

"Shouldn't we go back down?" Page inquired, smoothing back his cowlick. "They could still be alive. They might need—"

"Can't you see there's *nothing left of them!*" Del cried in despair.

Kyle tried to speak, but his lungs were encased in a barrel of ice.

"No way," Gillian whispered. "No way anyone could survive a fall like that."

"What are we going to *do*?" Lonny wailed, clutching himself. "We're lost up here, we're all alone! No one will ever find us!"

He and Lewis suddenly burst into tears, triggering a wave of moans from the other little ones. "We're just goners!" Lonny babbled on. "We're gonna die up here like the Donners did!"

"*Noooooo!*" Lewis screeched. He bolted down the path in a frenzy. Lissa and Marcus panicked and lit out into the brush.

"Hey, you come back here!" Del hollered. He jumped up and tore after Lewis.

Kyle and Gillian came to their senses and corralled Lissa and Marcus, herding them back to the group.

Dragging Lewis by the hand, Del strode to a protected hollow on the rocky summit. "All right, everybody over here!" The campers stumbled after him. Lewis huddled up against Kyle, shattered.

"Take it easy, Lewis," Kyle said, trying to comfort him. "We'll make it." Privately, he felt relieved that Del was taking charge.

"Now listen up and listen good." Del's features were pale and smeared with blood, but his eyes blazed. "We have plenty of provisions. We have tents and matches. We're *not* going to die. But we can't go back down. Gordon and Mr. Dugan are gone." His voice broke, then came back strong. "Do you understand? They're dead."

"What do you mean, we can't go back down?" Miles said, pulling his knitted cap over his flattop against the late afternoon chill. "Where else can we go?"

"Look." Del pointed to the horizon. "We're over halfway to Skyline Fireroad. It doesn't look that far anymore."

Kyle turned to the familiar notch in the Sierra crest. It did look close.

"Tomorrow night Sam will be there with the bus," Del continued. "But if we go back downhill, we'll have to hike at least forty miles to the first ranger station. It's just wilderness down there. Skyline Fireroad's our best shot."

"But we don't have maps," Gillian said. "None of us know

the way. You really think we can make it by tomorrow night?"

"Damn straight we can," Del replied. "We'll spend the night at those old prospectors' cabins near Lost Lake, just like Mr. Dugan said."

"We can follow the red tags," Kyle said.

Miles glared at him. "You're one to talk about red tags. We wouldn't be in this mess if you hadn't missed the tag and taken the wrong fucking path."

"I told you, there *was* no tag," Kyle protested.

"Bullshit! You're just lying to cover your ass."

"Hey, knock it off," Del said. "The accident's nobody's fault. It just happened."

Kyle looked at him in surprise. After capture the flag, he wouldn't have expected Del to stand up for anyone so untrustworthy.

"Teamwork is the key now," Del said, addressing everyone. "Remember that hokey Wolf Pack plaque in Mr. Dugan's office? Well, now it's for real—we *are* the Wolf Pack. The only way we're going to make it to the fireroad is by working together. That's the way Gordon and Mr. D would have wanted it." He wiped the blood from his face. "Now let's pack up and get the hell out of here. This place gives me the heebie-jeebies."

Del distributed the contents of Mr. Dugan's pack to the others, taking the burden of Gordon's load himself. Kyle gathered up the mountain-climbing equipment from the precipice.

Was the accident Gordon's fault? he wondered. *Had he tied a bad knot? Who cares whose fault it was?* Kyle's eyes burned. He moved to the lip of the precipice and peered down again at the body. It wasn't hard to imagine every bone and sinew crushed and torn. He began to sob.

Miles had been right, it *was* all his fault. He shouldn't have missed that red tag. He shouldn't have picked a path on impulse. He shouldn't have taken that dip in the mountain pool. He shouldn't have killed Marshall. Kyle closed his eyes and saw his brother lying underwater.

You're the one who should be down there in that tree, Kyle.

Kyle felt his throat close off; he choked and sputtered, fighting for breath, his heart pounding. He looked down and realized his feet were too close to the edge of the cliff. Taking that last step would be so simple, so right.

One foot in front of the other, soldier.

"Hey, Kyle!" Del's voice jarred him back to reality. "Let's get moving here."

Kyle eased back from the edge. Through his tears, he suddenly noticed that the horizon had disappeared under a thick, heavy ribbon of storm clouds. The word *stratocumulus* jolted to mind. Gordon had warned them about stratocumulus clouds, though it seemed ages ago. The angry, coalescing thunderheads were the sure sign of an approaching storm.

14

Gordon

Gordon's eyes popped open in bewilderment. Sharp-legged spiders skittering across his face had jolted him awake, but his groping fingers found nothing. He was sitting in his usual chair behind the movie projector in his classroom at Milwaukee Day School, a driver's-ed film unspooling on the old Bell & Howell. The room was dark and empty.

"The heat generated by the force of two automobiles colliding at sixty miles an hour is enough to fuse metal to metal on impact," the film's narrator intoned.

The screen showed the grisly aftermath of a passenger who had smashed through a windshield. "Had this unfortunate driver been wearing a seat belt—"

Gordon switched off the projector and struggled to remember what he was doing here. Maybe he had fallen asleep waiting for his students to arrive.

A gust of wind blew through an open window in a keen, irritating whine. Still disoriented, Gordon tried to get up and shut the window, but he couldn't move. A brassy chocolate taste suddenly filled his mouth. Why was the classroom swaying before him? Had he just awakened, or was this still part of a dream?

Where the blazes were his students? Gordon looked down to check his watch: It was unaccountably missing. What day was this, anyway? His head pounded with the force of a blacksmith's hammer against an anvil.

Jeez, I must have really tied one on last night.

On the projection table, he noticed a black plastic ball, a Magic Eight Ball toy. He hadn't seen one since childhood.

"Am I dreaming now?" he asked and shook the ball.

The answer floated up into the glass window: OUTLOOK NOT GOOD.

Footsteps echoed from the hall. Kyle Cody sauntered into the room, toting a driver's-ed manual.

"Kyle, where's the rest of the class?"

The boy did not answer. He snatched up the Magic Eight Ball and plopped down at a desk.

"Didn't you hear what I said? Where is everybody?"

Kyle ignored him, recklessly tossing the ball high in the air. The silly, wolfish grin on his face seemed out of character. He slumped back in his chair and tossed his leather cap on an empty desk. *Tap-tap-tap* went his foot against the chair leg.

"*Please* do not jiggle." All at once Gordon realized that Kyle was not one of his students, he was a camper at Wolf Gulch. "Wait a minute. What are you doing here, Kyle?"

"Checking you out, dude, what do you think?" Kyle replied with a sneer. He spoke in Billy Robin's voice.

Gordon's pulse began to beat at trip-hammer speed.

Freight train, freight train headache comin' round the bend, boomed a drunken voice in his head.

"Get out of here!" Gordon shouted. "You're not real."

"Who do you think you are?" Kyle jeered. "You're nothing. You're garbage."

"That's *enough!*"

Kyle abruptly hurled the Magic Eight Ball against the wall. It exploded in a shower of plastic shards and splattering water. The boy howled with laughter and marched out of the classroom.

Something gave suddenly in Gordon's chest. "Oh God," he moaned.

The brassy chocolate taste in his mouth liquefied into a warm flow that ran up onto his forehead, defying gravity. The invisible spiders began clawing at his face again.

They're eating me alive!

Gordon awoke with a terrified gasp. The spiders were sharp pine needles from a swaying bough. They slapped him full in the face, stinging his lips.

Where am I?

Paralyzed, Gordon looked down and saw storm clouds; overhead lay a boulder field. He was hanging upside down in a ponderosa pine, like a broken puppet. The tree swayed violently in an icy gust that whistled through the branches. Straining sideways, he picked out two fanglike buttes guarding a steep, rubble-covered mountain face.

What am I doing here?

Gordon had no recollection of what had happened. He was in The Wilds, that was all he knew. His bladder felt painfully full. But if he eliminated now he would douse himself in his own urine. He tried to right himself, straining against stabs of pain in his chest, but could not muster the strength to seize the branch overhead. Gordon hung helplessly, hyperventilating. He was scared and bewildered.

God help me. This is no dream.

The frayed Perlon climbing rope was wound unevenly around his chest. His parka and jeans were torn and ripped, bloody patches of flesh showing through the holes. He must have skidded down that granite washboard. The tree had saved his life.

Gordon began to remember. He had just delivered Kyle to the summit of the Dragonback. The others had thrown the rope down to Gordon. The rope somehow had given way. Why? Had his knot failed?

Get up.

He could not. It was easier to lie limp. He hawked and tried to spit out the warm chocolate taste lingering in his mouth. A dollop of bloody phlegm flew to the ground. *That means internal injuries,* he thought. His watch was missing, just as in the dream. It must have flown off during the fall.

Just get up, Gordon. Do it now or you'll die.

He ignored the stern voice in his head. But he could not neglect his need to urinate. It would be humiliating if the others found him dead in the tree, drenched in his own bodily fluids.

With pain-racked effort, Gordon finally seized hold of the branch and laboriously pulled himself up to a sitting position. Twenty feet separated him from the ground, and no lower limbs offered themselves. Gordon voided his bladder, legs dangling over the limb. The deep red color of his trickle of urine shocked him.

A violent image of Jerry Dugan tumbling down the Dragonback suddenly lurched into mind. *He must be nearby.* If Gordon had survived, why not Jerry too? A glance at the sun told him about two hours had passed since the accident. How long would it take for the campers to make it back down? Daylight would soon begin to fade.

Reality began to get a grip on him. What were his options? He had to find some way to climb down from the tree, that was the first priority. His responsibility to Jerry and the others came second but held greater weight. Hadn't he come back to The Wilds to prove he could prevail?

Gordon struggled to untangle the rope with renewed fervor. It wasn't until he slithered down and tumbled the last few feet to the ground that the entirety of the pain hit him. Every muscle and sinew in his body shrieked, and he collapsed on the shale-littered ground, the Dragonback spinning like a granite funnel before his eyes. *Better to die than endure this,* his mind screamed. He tucked his head between his knees and took deep, shuddering breaths.

Hold on, hold on.

Bursts of pain flared up at the slightest movement—and he wasn't even on his feet yet. Crouching in the lee of a boulder, Gordon took inventory of his injuries. The palms of his hands were bruised and raw. Something bobbed in his ribcage when he moved, and he was still coughing up blood. But the lacerations on his legs and torso were mercifully superficial. There were no broken bones, so he was ahead of the game.

Then he discovered the deep puncture wound on his calf. The sight of an opening so deep within his flesh made Gordon reel back, nauseous. He retched, splattering the ground with the undigested remains of his Spam sandwich, and fought back a mounting panic. Without survival gear, he didn't have a prayer overnight on this mountain. But there was no cause for alarm, not yet, he assured himself. The kids would show up any minute now, racing down the Dragonback to find him and Jerry. Wouldn't they?

Gordon took a long breath and rose shakily to his feet. If he could stand, he could walk. Holding onto a sapling for support, he scanned the rocks below.

"Jerry!" he cried, cupping his hands against the wind, his voice hoarse and cracked. "Jesus, where are you?"

Jerry had fallen from a greater height and therefore at a greater velocity. *Thirty-two feet per second per second,* his mind babbled. *That's tenth grade physics.* Whatever was left of Jerry had to be farther down the mountain.

Gordon released his grip on the tree and limped downhill. The broken rib, or whatever it was, quivered in his chest with every step. His legs turned to rubber, and another violent wave of nausea swept through him. He had underestimated the extent of his injuries. Weak and shuddering, Gordon crawled downhill on all fours, clambering over a mound of granite litter like a sick animal.

On the other side of the mound he found Jerry sprawled on top of a thick bush. He saw no blood, none of the gruesome driver's-ed-film injuries he had expected. The camp director looked strangely blissful, as if asleep. *Like Cal Wolcroft on last year's Ordeal,* Gordon thought with a shudder. He took Jerry's pulse and, to his relief, found a weak but steady heartbeat. Somehow, like Gordon, he had cheated death.

Gordon took him gently by the shoulders and eased him to the ground, then checked for injuries. Lacerations covered his arms and back. His hands were burned and bloody from the climbing rope. His hip did not feel right. Gordon pulled up Jerry's shirt. The flesh below his sacrum was purple and swollen, the bone broken and jutting out obliquely, stretching the skin around the open fracture. He would never be able to walk his way out of The Wilds. Gordon would have to drag him.

You can't do it, don't kid yourself. You can barely stand on your own two feet.

Gordon's eyes flitted back to the Dragonback. There was still no sign of the campers. They should have been here by now. Or had they given the two of them up for dead? Maybe he and Jerry were stranded in The Wilds without supplies or protection from the elements. The temperature was dropping, the trees casting elongated shadows. A night of exposure would finish them both off. Gordon shivered, more from despair than from the cold.

Don't try to lay the blame for this on The Wilds, Gordo. You did this to yourself.

His panic soared, his adrenaline pumping faster. "Dear God, please no," he begged in a whisper. Gordon curled up on the rock and hugged his trembling frame. His empty bladder strained to void again. Red dots danced before his eyes and he nearly blacked out.

Finally Gordon sat up, spent and weary. His panic ebbed, supplanted by a growing resolve. Since no one was going to rescue them, he had to count on himself to survive. This would be his test, the one Howard had told him about, the one he had come back for. He had his objective, but no means. How would he get the two of them out?

Your brain's your best survival gear.

Gordon struggled to his feet. The pain in his ribcage throbbed. He emptied his pockets, then ransacked Jerry's.

With shaking fingers he took stock of each item on a tree stump: one shotgun shell filled with precious tinder, a compass, a topographic map, a sealed bag of trail mix, a Swiss Army knife, nine hard candies, nineteen waterproof friction matches in a plastic container.

His shakes started up again. Gordon slowly recounted the matches to ease his mind, stalling the inevitable decision.

That's it, guy. Time to move out.

Their only chance was to catch up with the kids and make it to Skyline Fireroad before Sam's bus arrived. If the campers had given them up for dead, they would be trying to find Lost Lake and the prospectors' cabins. Could he and Jerry reach Lost Lake before nightfall?

A bone-chilling gust of wind swept down from the Sierra crest.

Gordon set to cutting pine boughs with his knife to build a makeshift litter for Jerry. He wondered how that red tag could have ended up in his pocket. He had absolutely no recollection of taking it.

15

Del

Del led the way up a narrow path littered with slippery slag detritus. A set of ivory peaks, dead ahead, cast deep afternoon shadows over the campers, robbing them of sunlight. They had ascended a good thousand feet in just two hours. It seemed they were fast approaching the highest pass in the Sierra crest. Del's feet were so sore that he could feel every stone through the thick Vibram soles of his boots. The others were exhausted, but they just kept plodding on. Del was proud of them.

"Not too far to the top, guys," Del yelled over his shoulder. He was huffing from the added weight of Gordon's gear. "Lost Lake coming up."

"How much longer?" Lewis asked, dragging his pack on the ground behind him.

"Soon," Del promised. "Don't do that with your pack, Lewis. That won't make it any lighter." He wondered if the frail boy had the stamina to finish the trek.

On the horizon the black sky was shot with ribbons of purple. Del gazed wearily at the rocky expanse of the defied, glacier-scoured pass. Billowy slate-gray clouds were piling in around the summits. Those clouds worried him. He tried to remember the winding contours of Gordon's topographic map. If they didn't reach the summit soon, these kids weren't going to make it.

Del glanced back at Kyle, who was shepherding the slower kids at the rear, urging them to keep up with Del's grueling pace. Kyle hadn't been this determined or cooperative since the canoe joust. Maybe the two of them were still a team after all. Earlier, Kyle had pointed out the clouds, reminding everyone of Gordon's warning. They had to find those prospectors' cabins quickly.

An impatient burst of energy powered Del on. Abandoning the switchback trail, he cut a steep beeline directly toward the pass. Sharp chunks of loose rock scraped at his ankles. He didn't stop until he reached the crest, the end of their agony. His breath stopped short.

"Oh Christ."

It was a false summit, a lie. Beyond lay ridge after brutish ridge, each successively higher—a jumbled file that faded into the cloudy horizon. In a small valley below, four tiny lakes glistened like teardrops on green felt.

Four lakes?

"Way to go, Rambo," Miles said, squatting next to him to catch his breath. "I thought you said we were—"

"Well, we're not, okay? I'm just doing the best I can here." As Gillian and the older boys struggled up to join them, Del pointed out a serpentine tracing that looped up a draw and laced around a glacial moraine. "That's our path. Got to be."

"You mean we have to go uphill *again*?" Gillian asked in disbelief.

Del nodded. "Okay, let's move out. Lost Lake should be on the other side of that rise."

Kyle and the rear ranks arrived, the younger campers exhausted. "How're we doing?" Kyle asked, trying to sound chipper.

"We're not," Miles replied.

"When are we going to get there?" Lonny said.

"I'm tired," Lewis announced, collapsing to the ground. "I can't walk anymore."

"Neither can I," Jennifer said and sat on a rock, dumping her pack. "I *quit*."

"I thought you were all big kids," Del said, pacing about, gathering up a second wind. "Guess I was wrong."

"I'm not tired," Page protested, still on his feet. "I could go on for miles. It's simply mind over matter."

But the other little kids mewled and groaned, crouching crablike on the granite, refusing to budge.

Del didn't know what to do. "Come *on* now, let's shake a leg here," he said, trying to sound like Mr. Dugan. He turned to Kyle imploringly. "Help me get them up, will you?"

Kyle shrugged. "What can I do, Del? They're beat."

"You quitting on me too?"

"Not me. I'm ready to boogie."

"Del's right," Gillian said. "We have to keep moving." No one moved. "Hey, don't forget I'm deputy counselor here," she added. "Mr. Dugan said so."

"Why can't we just camp here?" Haines asked, collapsing against a boulder.

Miles remained in a recalcitrant squat. "Fuck it, man, I'm dead."

"No shit," Frank agreed, joining them. Only Del, Kyle, Gillian, and little Page remained standing.

Del narrowed his eyes on the three boys. "I didn't expect you guys to be such pussies. I said *get up*! Nobody quits until *I* say so." His voice climbed. "On your feet, ladies!"

Reluctantly Miles, Haines, and Frank struggled up. Del's self-confidence held strong; he was still the leader here. "You too, small fries," he added. "You don't want that Donner Man to get you, do you?"

The campers trekked slowly up a steep escarpment, following the trail of red tags. The path dwindled to nothing in the crumbled talus. The wind increased, forcing the hikers to drop their heads and lean into it. Skyline Fireroad and the peaks were lost in the darkening wall of approaching clouds.

Del led on relentlessly, daring neither to stop to don warmer clothes, nor slow the pace.

"Del?" It was Gillian, trying to match his die-hard pace. "Don't you think we'd better set up the tents?" She glanced at the clouds. "I'm getting worried."

"Me too."

"Then let's stop. I do have some hiking experience, you know. My gut feeling says we should make camp now."

Del shook his head.

"Del, we'll never make it to Lost Lake."

"Of course we will." He fixed his eyes on the top of a humpbacked cirque covered with wildflowers. "It's got to be on the other side of that rise."

"You've been saying that every time we come to a new hill."

"Show a little faith, why don't you."

Gillian did not answer.

Coming over the top of the rise, Del caught sight of a rippling expanse of turquoise water.

"See!" he hollered. "We did it!"

He fairly bounded down the hill, dancing through the patches of wild onion and meager stands of willow along the edge of the kidney-shaped lake.

"Far fucking out!" Miles cried enthusiastically, galloping down to join him. Their boots sank into the boggy swale at the lake's edge. The others followed at a struggling gait and crowded around Del.

"So where are the cabins?" Page asked, eyeing the shoreline.

"We'll find them," Del said. They set off along a path bordering the water, now taking the time to pull on sweaters, hats, and gloves. Miles followed a parallel route higher up the slope. Nearing the far end of the lake, Del's confidence began to wane.

"Hey! Over here," shouted Miles from a higher path, jabbing his finger at something beyond their view. "I see them."

Everyone clambered up the incline to join him. The corner of a small stone structure came into sight and everyone cheered. Del led the way to the cabin, breaking into a run. He shoved open the old wooden door. It fell off its hinges with a dull thud of rotted timber.

The cabin had no roof. Del stared down in dismay at the debris littering the exposed cabin floor: rocks and chunks of lime mortar, faded Coors beer cans, rusty mining equipment, an ancient wagon wheel that looked as old as the gold rush. Del hid his trembling hands in his pockets.

"This can't be the right place," Gillian said, peering inside with the others.

"Of course it is. The roof fell in, that's all."

"Yeah, in about 1950," Miles said.

"We can still make camp here," Del insisted with forced bravado.

"Hey, aren't there supposed to be *two* cabins?" Page said. "This just can't be Lost Lake, Del. Let's face it, we're not on the right trail. We're lost."

Del heaved off his pack. "Lost Lake or not, Professor, this is where we're camping. You guys help me clear out some of these big rocks. Then we'll string the tents up from those old beams. Now let's get cracking."

No one protested; the alternative of trekking onward was too daunting. Del and Kyle found a couple of ancient rusty mining picks and used them as crowbars to pry the larger rocks loose. Gillian and the others piled the rubble against the foundation of a half-collapsed wall.

Jennifer and Lewis joined in to lift a basketball-sized rock together. They dropped it suddenly, screaming.

Del rushed over. "What's the problem?"

Part of a human pelvis had tumbled out of the rubble. As Del examined it, the brown withered bones crumbled apart in his hands.

"The Donner Party!" Lonny wailed.

"This must be where it actually *happened*," Jennifer exclaimed in hushed awe.

"Where what happened?" Page said.

"Where they *ate* each other, stupid—the Donners!"

The other little ones reared back in fright. "Don't be ridiculous," Page countered with a smirk. "Those bones aren't that old. Besides, the Donners didn't drink Coors from the can, did they?"

Lonny and Lewis turned and fled outside. The rest of the little ones quickly followed.

"Come on, you guys," Gillian called after them. "You're being silly."

"This is just great," Del said, hands on his hips.

"Maybe we better just push on," Kyle suggested. "No way those kids are going to camp here."

Del knew Kyle was right. He felt something cold splatter on his forehead. He raised his face skyward. Snowflakes, white and fluffy, were capering down in the whipping wind.

The snow fell gently at first, whitening the treetops. The veil of flurries obscured only the highest palisades and peaks. Then a crystalline topping began to collect on the rocks like powdered sugar. It was a deceptively picturesque scene from a Christmas card.

To Del, trudging onward, the fluffy, pristine beauty promised no celebration. This was *June.* These light-spirited snowflakes signified nothing less than a threat to everyone's survival. Summer snowstorms were unusual, Del knew, but not unheard of at these altitudes. Gordon had been right. The Wolf Gulch Ordeal should have been postponed.

After leaving the ruined cabin, the campers had backtracked a mile from the lake and found the right trail. Del couldn't be blamed; it had been an understandable mistake. Those red tags, posted in profusion where the path was clear, seemed to vanish when the trail grew hard to follow. Now surely Lost Lake must be close at hand.

But the path was rapidly disappearing under snow. The campers would have to bushwhack soon, without a path. Should they chance it, or should they dig in somewhere for the night? But dig in *where*? Despite the late afternoon chill, a rivulet of sweat dripped down Del's temple. If he made another mistake, his credibility would be nil.

Del glanced back at his bedraggled caravan of campers, stumbling over rocks already slippery with sleet. Ice flakes were already congealing on everyone's parkas.

The snowfall slowly, almost imperceptibly, increased; even the flakes grew thicker. Nearby stands of Jeffrey pines vanished behind the veil of wind-driven snow. Thick, sticky snowflakes clung persistently to Del's eyebrows and the fake fur collar of his parka; they sifted down the back of his sweater. They hounded him, peppering his face.

Just let us find those cabins, Del prayed, squinting his eyes to ward off the snow's assault.

Before long, a howling wind began blowing from all points of the compass, whipping the snow into a fury. A milky whiteness blanketed the ground, the sky, obliterating every shadow.

Del slowed his pace, losing all vision and sense of perspective in the whiteout. It was impossible to judge the terrain—he couldn't even see beyond the next footstep.

"Look," he shouted, pointing at a rusty cylinder just ahead. "An oil drum! The cabins must be close now."

Del soon realized his mistake. It was only an empty soup can half-buried in the snow just twenty feet away. He had completely misjudged it. He crushed the can out of sight under his heel and pressed on before the others could catch up.

Del took a step forward—and his boot kept going down. Below lay empty, translucent space. He was teetering on the brink of some kind of crevasse. Waving his arms like windmill sails, he recovered his balance just as Gillian and Kyle materialized from the whiteout. A gust of wind propelled his cap high into the white oblivion.

"Crevasse!" he cried. "Watch out!" Del stared down into the mouth of the maw that blocked their path. It was another major setback. "We'll have to backtrack again. We're completely cut off by this thing."

"That's *enough*," Miles said, panting. "I'm cashing it in right here."

"I've had it too," Gillian said in defeat. "I'm not going anywhere."

The little kids slumped in the snow, too tired to bawl.

"Where's Kyle?" Page asked.

No one seemed to know or care.

"Come on, Wolf Pack," Del said, his voice rising. "Move out!"

Nobody budged. Flustered, Del wiped his ice-caked face and searched the campers' eyes for some sign of cooperation. "Come on now. Gordon and Mr. Dugan would be ashamed if they saw you like this."

Kyle suddenly appeared from the swirling snow. "I found an overhang," he said, flushed and excited. "It's big enough for all of us. Come on."

Before Del had a chance to respond, everyone moved after Kyle into the whiteout. Del followed.

Kyle led them to a rocky outcrop, an overhang where drifting snow had formed walls, creating a pocket of protection from the elements.

Without a word, Kyle slipped through the opening. The others quickly crawled in after him, one at a time. Del heard a sharp report some distance above them. He held back.

"Hey, wait a second. We're right under an avalanche track. We could all be buried alive in there."

"I'll take my chances, blood," Miles said.

For a moment, Jennifer and a few others hesitated. But they were too exhausted and desperate to heed Del's warning.

"Come on, Del," Gillian said, motioning him inside.

Del shook his head. "If there's an avalanche, who's going to dig you out? I'll stay out here and keep watch."

Gillian shrugged wearily and wriggled out of sight. Haines was the last to move inside, carrying the food packs.

"Haines," Del called out to him. "Make sure no one touches the grub until morning. Tell Kyle. Understand?"

The boy nodded and disappeared, leaving Del alone in the storm. The whiteout had turned gray; dusk was falling. He knelt in the snow, struggling to erect his tent between gusts of wind. The snow on the mountain overhead cracked again loudly, a foreboding sound.

The mountain wants us dead and buried.

But Del wouldn't let that happen. Despite their foolishness, he would make sure the others were safe. Though cold and lonely, Del took comfort in the certainty that they would soon realize the value of his leadership, the importance of his selfless sacrifice for the good of the group. He knew he was doing the right thing.

16

Gordon

The snow came down at a steep, wind-driven angle. Gordon staggered up the slippery Dragonback, hauling Jerry's heavy travois, glancing repeatedly at the snow clouds in shock and disbelief. The blizzard had come out of nowhere, transforming The Wilds into a white wasteland.

Goddamnit! Didn't I warn you about this, Jerry? Didn't I, you greenhorn?

Gordon's breath came in shrill convulsive gasps; his wounds throbbed. Jerry was still unconscious, his face glazed with ice particles. The two of them absolutely had to make it to the top of the Dragonback before the trail disappeared.

Gordon used whatever he could to keep himself going. He thought of Howard DeRosa and imagined his friend cajoling him, encouraging him, pushing him to take one more step, then another. He would feel guilty if he let Howard down.

Onward and upward.

The icy wind slashed at his chapped face. He gripped the tow rope tightly with numbed hands. The litter sloughed sideways on the sleet-covered switchback, and he paused to sweep the accumulated snow off Jerry, who lay so lifelessly on the litter. In the twilight, the looming Dragonback had melted into a dark outline, indistinct and menacing.

A white-throated swift began singing its *jeejeejeejeejee* song in a frivolous, mocking tone.

What are you doing out in this shitstorm, little bird?

He kept his eyes riveted on the fading path before him, his body leaning over his boots against the weight of Jerry's litter.

Andele, andele.

The path suddenly leveled out beneath him, and Gordon fell forward, smacking his chin on a rock. After a stunned moment, he realized that he had reached the top. Windborne snow billowed like a tumbling cataract over the lip of the Dragonback. Gordon stumbled across the promontory to the fissured boulder where he had secured the climbing rope. Had his knot failed, or had the boulder moved? There was no way to know.

As Gordon had expected, the campers were gone. They had given their counselors up for dead and moved on for the fireroad. Had they left any food behind, any stray gear? A quick search uncovered the snow-caked wrappers of four Mars bars and a rusty, long-abandoned tin cup. The candy wrappers yielded two crumbs of chocolate that vanished like ghosts on his greedy tongue, leaving only a memory of the taste. It struck Gordon how quickly man could become a scavenger, a vulture picking through refuse. Thinking ahead, he carefully pocketed the cup.

A voice welled up from behind: "Oh my Christ! In the name of God!"

Gordon whipped around. Jerry was writhing on the litter, shaking violently. Gordon knelt and held him down. Chunks of rime ice had crystallized in Jerry's sideburns. His skin felt far too cold—a dead man's flesh. The older man mumbled and cursed deliriously to himself. His heartbeat was irregular, his respiration slow. This was first-stage hypothermia; Gordon recognized the symptoms.

The camp director's eyes suddenly opened and rolled wildly. "... *Donner Party, gaaa* ..." he mumbled, delirious. "... *mmmmm man.*"

Gordon thought he heard the words *Mr. Man* and flinched in astonishment. He grabbed Jerry's shoulder and jostled him. "Jerry! What did you say?"

Jerry's efforts to speak triggered a rasping cough that sounded almost like a sinister cackle. His eyes rolled back into his head and he passed out again.

Collecting himself, Gordon knew he would have to act

quickly to save him. Jerry's core temperature was dropping close to the point where his body could no longer rewarm itself; the brain was restricting blood flow to the extremities. Without warmth, Jerry's cardiac and respiratory centers would fail. Cardiac fibrillation and edema would ensue, and the lungs would hemorrhage. Death would follow swiftly.

Gordon spotted a sparse stand of conifers in a rocky recess sheltered from the wind. As he dragged the travois over to the trees, the white-throated swift flew in a circle overhead, mocking them with its jeering cry.

Gonna get you out of this, Jer. I swear I will.

A fallen fir provided the main support beam for Gordon's shelter. He cut as many pine boughs as he could reach with his knife and lay them against the beam. The boughs were not enough, and he piled on a layer of insulating snow. The work took longer than he had anticipated; his throat was parched with thirst. He was tempted to eat a handful of snow. No, he decided, that would only lower his own body temperature.

"Almost ready, Jer."

Jerry couldn't hear him, but there was comfort in the sound of his own voice. He crawled inside the lean-to. On all fours, he scooped away the snow, pushing it out between his legs until he hit mineral earth. He lined the shelter with more pine boughs. By the time he ducked back outside, Jerry was again already half-covered with spindrift.

"You weigh a ton, Jer," he said as he dragged the inert form inside. Jerry's head lolled back, jaw slack. "Don't worry, you *are* going to make it."

He buried Jerry in a cocoon of bark and the last of the pine boughs. Squatting, he dug a small pit in the freezing earth with his tin cup, then fashioned a mound of twigs and pine needles. After cutting a small chimney hole, he took the firestarter kit from his parka, savoring the odor of the kerosene-soaked steel wool; it reminded him of civilization. The match ignited and a tiny flame jumped onto the needles. Gordon fed the small blaze slowly, making sure the fire did not melt the snow walls or set fire to the pine boughs. He pulled Jerry's litter against the open door, sealing them inside.

The shelter immediately began to warm. Gordon looked around with satisfaction, allowing himself a moment to relax. This had been a day to remember. He had been tossed down a mountain, battered and frozen to the bone, stripped of his gear, and abandoned for dead. But he had kept both of them alive this far. If he stayed up all night feeding the fire, as firetenders had done for centuries, they would survive. In the morning, they would catch up with the campers. The nightmare would be over.

He melted snow in the cup, stirring in a hard candy, and pressed it to Jerry's lips.

"Come on, Jer. Give yourself a chance here."

The hot liquid trickled uselessly down the older man's collar.

"Okay, I'll give you some time to warm up first. Then we'll try it again."

Gordon moved closer to the fire, rolled up his damp jeans, and checked the deep puncture wound on his calf. It was inflamed and suppurating. Without antibiotics, an abscess could develop. He recounted his matches, then ate a handful of trail mix washed down with the hot sweetened water. Revived, Gordon went out for firewood. He returned to check Jerry, whose hands, throat, and abdomen were still much too cold. Jerry was in deep hypothermia. His body had cooled through to the core. No fire would save him now. Gordon had to do something fast.

He tugged Jerry over on his back and stripped him naked. His clothes were wet and crusted with ice; they had the consistency of starched laundry. Gordon hung them on sticks around the fire and quickly tossed off his own clothing. He slipped under the boughs and wrapped himself around Jerry's shivering body. Skin against skin, arms and legs entwined, Gordon felt his own warmth ebb, absorbed by the frigid form next to him, and he shivered violently. There was nothing more he could do now. Whatever would happen would happen.

As he held Jerry tightly, the mystery of the missing red tag returned to plague Gordon's thoughts.

It suddenly occurred to him that *Del* could have done it. Angry at Gordon for chastising him, upset with Kyle, Del had taken the tag to get even with them both. Planting it in Gordon's pocket was part of the plan, the revenge. The hypothesis was possible, but still farfetched.

So I'm back where I started. Did I or didn't I?

The idea that he might have taken it with no recollection of the act troubled him deeply. What could have possessed him? To deliberately lead Kyle off the trail? The idea was absurd. He genuinely liked Kyle. The kid reminded him of himself as a boy, and that moment with the buck had sealed the connection between them. He would never knowingly do anything to hurt Kyle.

He would never hurt anyone.

Not even Billy Robin? a sarcastic voice asked in his head. Gordon buried his face on Jerry's raw, palpitating chest. He began to weep.

17

Kyle

Kyle awoke from a dreamless sleep to the playful sounds of children shouting and giggling.

Sunlight streamed through a translucent wall of dripping, ice-slicked snow. Some of the others were gathered around him in their sleeping bags, still asleep. Kyle stood up painfully; eight hours on the rocky floor had rearranged his spine. Nobody had slept well; the little kids' persistent complaints about the cold had kept everyone up most of the night.

He crawled through the opening, emerging onto a sunny plateau cloaked in a knee-deep mantle of fresh snow. The drifts appeared six feet deep or more. It was hard to believe how much snow had fallen overnight. The sky was a fierce, purple-tinged shade of blue dappled by a few harmless puffs of cumulus; near the horizon, it was the color of fresh lime. For the first time, Kyle could clearly see their position midway up a steep, wind-fretted snowfield. The abyss that had blocked their way the night before could be skirted by hiking a hundred feet uphill.

The snowfield glittered harshly in the sunlight. Del's tent was barely visible, completely encased in a drift. Down the incline, behind them, lay a stark blue corner of the unknown lake they had passed yesterday. Ahead loomed the distinctive notch of Skyline Fireroad. Del may not have found the exact trail, but he had nearly pulled them through, halving the distance to the pickup point.

Kyle followed the children's voices and slogged through the knee-high snow. He found the kids sledding down a rolling slope on plastic garbage bags.

"Man, that was an E-ticket ride," Marcus cried.

Jennifer was lying on her back in the snow, giggling. "This is Smurfy! I never want to go home."

"I do," Lonny said. "Beam me up, Scotty. I miss Alf and Pee-wee Herman. And Egg McMuffins."

"That's so philistine," Page protested.

Kyle struggled his way over to the sledders. "Hey guys, that's not such a good idea. There could be an avalanche or something."

The kids glared at Kyle resentfully and promptly ignored him. Kyle shrugged them off and returned to the campsite. Frank was up, working through a regimen of calisthenics outside the overhang in a depression of flattened snow. Gillian was sitting on a plastic tarp, warming snow in a pot over the Coleman stove.

"Morning," Kyle said, a little too formally, bending down to warm his hands.

"Hi there. Want cocoa or coffee?"

"Coffee, please." Kyle admired the hale, ruddy effect the cold had on Gillian's cheeks. Her hair looked better tousled and uncombed, he decided. Back at camp, she had always come off so impeccably well-groomed. He smiled at her torn, sodden parka, her filthy jeans, the smudges on her forehead. "You look terrific," he said, gulping his coffee. "Sort of wild and woolly."

"Right." Gillian rolled her eyes. "I've been avoiding my pocket mirror. I'd make a great cover girl for *Field & Stream.*"

Kyle nodded toward Del's half-buried tent. "Looks like he's sleeping in."

"Guess Del had a pretty rough night."

"Guess we all did." Kyle watched the water boil. "There's a better way to melt snow."

"Not in this cold."

"Yeah? Watch this." Kyle borrowed the plastic tarp and piled a conical mound of snow in the center.

"That'll take forever," Gillian protested.

"Want to bet?"

In less than a minute, beads of water started collecting on the plastic.

"This will save on Coleman gas, too," Kyle said.

"Where'd you learn that?" she asked, surprised.

"Saw it on TV once. A *National Geographic* special."

"I'll have to teach that to my dad next time he takes me hiking."

"Family outing, huh?"

She shook her head. "Just the two of us. He's divorced."

"Mine too," Kyle said with a commiserating smile.

Gillian's mood darkened. "I dreamt about the accident last night. Couldn't shake it loose."

"Funny, I didn't dream about anything," Kyle said with a twinge of remorse. "I think about it a lot, though."

Gillian shuddered. "It was awful."

"Yeah. I was never more scared in my life. I feel so shitty about it."

"You shouldn't."

"Especially about Gordon. Gordon was a great guy. Dugan was okay too."

"There was nothing we could have done about it," Gillian said.

"I guess."

"I never saw a person die before."

Kyle said nothing, retreating into his thoughts.

"I hope to God I never have to see anyone die again."

Gillian poured the coffee. "You think we'll have to come back here to help the police—the mountain rescue guys?"

"You mean to find the counselors' bodies after we're rescued?"

She nodded.

"I don't know. Probably."

"I don't want to come back here again. Ever."

Del's snowbound tent suddenly began to shake, the snowdrift falling away.

"Where is everybody?" came Del's voice as he emerged from the tent, his eyes red and swollen. "Hey, get off of there!" he shouted to the little kids on the slope. "Let's go dig into some breakfast."

Del waded through the snow to the overhang, the kids in tow. "Everybody *up!*" he bellowed. Then he noticed Kyle, Gillian, and Frank. "That wasn't too swift, guys," he said, joining them. "You shouldn't have let them go tobogganing by themselves."

"Hey man, it's not *my* problem," Frank said, doing deep knee bends.

"It's everybody's problem. They could have—"

"Yeah, I know," Kyle interrupted. "They could have started an avalanche." He grinned. "Turn around, Del. Look up the mountain."

"Huh?"

"Skyline Fireroad. We've cut the distance in half. We may be off the trail, but your homing instincts were right on. And we can go right around that big crevasse."

"Well what do you know." Del gazed up at their destination. "We're just hours away now."

"I don't know," Gillian wondered aloud. "Distances can be deceiving. Remember what Gordon said."

Little Lonny tugged at Del's sleeve. "Del? Del?"

"Yeah, what?"

"I'm hungry. I want some *real* food—I'm sick of trail mix."

"No problem." Del turned to Miles and Haines, who were climbing sleepily out of the overhang. "Hey Miles, go get those food packs from inside, will you?"

Miles complied.

Page stretched and observed the clear skies. "Ah, wilderness," he said, waxing grandiloquently. "Once again Indiana Jones and his faithful band of explorers have come through another night of raging death and destruction—"

"Button it, you worm," Frank said between jumping jacks.

"I had this horrible nightmare," Lonny told Marcus. "A monster was chasing me—like the mummy in that old horror movie. Only it had snot and brains hanging out of its skull. The thing just came at me, and I couldn't move!"

"Must have been that old Donner Man," Jennifer taunted.

Miles suddenly scrambled out of the overhang. "Somebody's opened almost all the food!" he shouted. "The little kids must've been snacking while we all slept. Stuff's spread all over the fucking place."

Del blanched. "Haines, didn't you tell Kyle to watch the packs?"

"We were all asleep," Haines said.

"Goddamnit, Haines."

"Hey, Del, you were sleeping too," Gillian protested.

"No, Del's right," Kyle said. "We should've kept better tabs on what was going on."

"All right," Del decided, "it's not the end of the world. Long as we make it to the fireroad."

"I'm not putting any bets on it," Miles said.

Del gave him a sizzling glance. "Shut up, Miles."

"Hey, where's Lewis?" Jennifer asked.

"Still asleep inside," Miles said.

"Somebody go wake him up," Del ordered. Then he changed his mind. "Forget it, I'll do it myself. I don't want anybody else in that avalanche trap." He turned to the overhang, gesturing at the melting snow above the opening.

"Look at this! It's just *asking* for a disaster." He ducked inside.

Miles shook his head with a snicker. "Rambo's sure got a nail up his butt today."

"Can it, Miles," Kyle said.

"Hey, what's your problem?"

"He's just doing his job. All you ever do is bitch."

Miles faced him off. "Yeah? And what are you going to do about it?"

Moments later Del scrambled back out, stricken. "Something's wrong with Lewis. He won't wake up."

The others rushed into the shelter after Del. It took Kyle a moment to realize he was looking at a dead body. Rigor mortis had locked the frail little boy in a fetal position.

Kyle bent down and could see frost on Lewis's eyebrows. He backed away, shaken.

Del opened Lewis's jacket and laid his head on the boy's chest, listening for a heartbeat.

"Del," Gillian said finally, wiping back tears. "I don't think you need to do that... ."

"I know." Del's voice quavered. "I'm just making sure."

Kyle gazed blankly at the wasted food packets scattered on the cave floor.

Del rose and wiped his eyes. "I think we'd better leave. This place is a better tomb than we could ever dig for him."

The campers filed dumbly out into the sunlight.

"We should mark the location," Gillian muttered. "After we're rescued, they'll want to come back for the body."

"Maybe *we'll* want the body," Miles said, but this time he wasn't joking. "Like the Donner Party."

Del whirled around, grabbed Miles by the shoulders, and hurled him to the ground. Then his shoulders sagged. Del shuffled to his tent and disappeared inside.

18

Gordon

"Shouldn't we get going soon, Gordon?"

The familiar voice nudged Gordon from a deep sleep. He lingered in that twilight world between consciousness and the dream state, vaguely aware that he did not *want* to wake up. There was safety in sleep, in dreaming, where he lay entwined with a voluptuous woman whose name he did not know. She radiated all the warmth of the womb, and he snuggled tightly against her, basking gratefully in her heat.

"I say, there. We're getting awfully familiar here, aren't we?"

The merry, male voice made Gordon open his eyes in confusion. An owlish face stared back at him. Gordon pulled back abruptly from Jerry's naked body. He sat up, embarrassed, breaking away from the warm layer of bark and pine needles.

"Sorry," he said thickly, collecting himself. "Must have been dreaming."

Jerry was lying on his side. His face was drawn and blanched. "I was hoping I'd feel better today."

"You were freezing last night. You had hypothermia. I thought you were going to pack it in, so I stripped you down. Had to warm you up any way I could." Gordon grinned suddenly. It seemed like weeks since he'd spoken to another human being.

Jerry looked around their primitive shelter. "I wish we were back at Wolf Gulch. A nice cozy cabin, hot soup. Say, chunky beef soup with rice. Wouldn't mind that a bit."

"You're lucky you didn't warm up too fast, actually," Gordon said.

"Come again?"

"When you're coming out of deep hypothermia, the brain pumps blood to your cold extremities. That cools the blood, of course, and the blood cools the major organs. If you'd gotten warm too quickly, you could have gone out on me, Jer."

Jerry smiled weakly, revealing a fractured tooth from his fall. "I guess I'm still here, no small thanks to you." He touched Gordon's arm. "You saved my life, Gordon."

Gordon pressed his hand. "Hey, you would've done the same for me."

"We fell down the Dragonback, didn't we?"

"You remember it?"

Jerry shook his head. "During the night, I started remembering bits and snatches of you hauling me back up the path, so I deduced the rest. Are you hurt?"

"A broken rib, I think. Not too bad, considering."

"What about me?"

"We have to get you to a hospital. You're still on pretty shaky ground, Jer." *Didn't I warn you?* he wanted to add. *Didn't I try to tell you what to expect from this place?*

"Did the campers go back for help?" Jerry asked.

"Doesn't look like it."

"I don't understand."

"I think they're trying to make it to Skyline Fireroad. Problem is, with the snow obscuring those red tags, they'll be off-trail by now. If the Forest Service sends in a rescue team, they'll never find those kids. Not until it clears enough to send in choppers, anyway."

"I'm very worried about them, Gordie."

"Let's worry about ourselves right now."

Gordon pushed open the pine bough door. The bright sunlight made him squint. Leaning outside, he saw incisor-like peaks against naked blue sky. The drifted snow looked deep, but the weather had cleared. And their makeshift shelter had survived the night. If Gordon had to, he would build another one today, farther up the trail.

"We'd better get moving if we want to catch up with those kids today," he said, moving back inside.

"Of course." Jerry made a feeble attempt to dress but could barely move.

Gordon leaned over him. "Let's take a peek at that hip."

The skin around Jerry's open fracture was acutely inflamed. The edges of the wound near the bone were black, while the entire leg had turned the brownish color of a blood blister.

Gordon poked a finger into his calf. "Feel that?"

"Barely. I don't like the looks of it, though. Think I'll be okay?"

The skin still showed the mark of Gordon's fingertip. Jerry's leg had devitalized from lack of blood flow. Gordon put his palm to the older man's forehead.

"I've got a touch of fever, haven't I?"

Gordon nodded, deliberating quickly. Jerry's only chance was an air rescue within the next twenty-four hours. Even then he would lose the leg, no question. Should he tell the truth, or was it kinder to lie?

Remember what happened to Pop Hollos.

After Dad's exploratory surgery, it had been up to Gordon to make a decision. He hadn't had the heart to tell Dad how seriously the cancer had metastasized. It was kinder, he had thought, to let him enjoy his last few months without worrying what the end would be like. *How much pain will there be? Will the morphine kill it?* Those were questions Dad shouldn't have had to face until the time came.

But after the second operation, when his father came out of anesthesia, Gordon couldn't look him in the eye. Pop Hollos was a gaunt husk of himself. The surgeon had bypassed his stomach, feeding him on predigested liquids pumped into him through tubes.

Dad couldn't speak, but he stared at Gordon. Gone was that demanding, sardonic critic. *What are they doing to me, Gordie?* those feeble, bewildered eyes asked. *Tell me what my chances are, for the love of God!*

Gordon had cheated Dad out of confronting death. He had vowed he would never deceive anyone like that again.

"You've got Clostridia, Jerry. I'm pretty sure of it."

Jerry's eyes flickered. "Sounds nasty. What is it?"

"Gas gangrene. Serious stuff."

"You're sure?"

"I've read about it in survival manuals," Gordon said.

"Bad, huh? Am I going to lose the leg?"

Their eyes met. Unlike Dad's eyes, Jerry's were clear and lucid.

"I think so," Gordon said slowly. "But it might be worse than losing a leg. Toxins from the gangrene zip right into the bloodstream and they spread through the body quickly. I think that's causing your fever."

"It's already happening, then. I'm dying, that's what you're telling me."

Gordon could only nod.

Jerry gripped his hand firmly. "Let's make a pact, then. When I pack it in, you go on after the kids right away. No burial, no eulogy. They need your help, Gordon, as much as we need theirs. We have a responsibility to their parents."

"I know that. Del will do all right by them, I really think he will."

"*Promise* me, Gordon, right now. Are we agreed?"

"Agreed," said Gordon, squeezing his hand. "I won't let you down."

"I know you won't."

Gordon turned to hide the tears in his eyes. "We'd better get going."

He busied himself gathering chunks of charcoal from the dead firepit. They did not speak as he tied Jerry onto the litter. The camp director remained quiet and withdrawn, driven deep into himself.

Gordon stood still for a moment, gauging the terrain. The trail appeared to traverse a steep ridge, but deep drifts made it impassable. Which way should he go? Had the kids made it to Lost Lake or were they lost somewhere, far from the path? Though he had hiked this trail before, Gordon did not know the way by heart, nor had he ever experienced The Wilds under snow. He would have to depend almost entirely on the topographic map, hoping luck and gut instinct would pull them through.

He decided to follow the crest of the ridge, where wind had swept away most of the snowfall.

"Head 'em up, move 'em out," he said, trying to sound cheerful. The day's trek had begun.

The ridge meandered uphill around snow-bearded turrets of black, bulging rock. At first Gordon felt new, determined energy flowing through his body. The clear skies and bright sunlight lifted his spirits. But it was his promise to Jerry that drove him relentlessly onward. Maybe today Wolf Gulch would send in a search-and-rescue chopper. Jerry could be in a hospital by noon.

Gordon realized he was starting to perspire and slowed down, pacing himself. *Ration your sweat, not your water,* so the saying went. Sweaty clothing could stiffen and freeze when the body cooled.

"Stop!" Jerry shouted. "Look." He pointed excitedly at a bright splash of orange in the snow.

Gordon picked up an empty Fritos bag and grinned delightedly. "If we can keep up this pace, we'll reach them by nightfall."

Moments later, Gordon spotted a crimson splash of color waving spritely from a lodgepole pine—a red tag. But at the bottom of a bowl-shaped declivity, off to the east, lay an empty Mars bar wrapper.

"We'd better go into the bowl," he said. "Looks like the kids never got to Lost Lake. They veered off here."

Jerry grunted his assent.

Gordon started downhill, playing tug-of-war with the towrope to keep Jerry's litter from sliding too fast. After a few hundred feet he was up to his knees in snow, then to his thighs. By the time Gordon reached the far side and started uphill again, his lungs were burning. Jerry's litter had grown intolerably heavy, and the altitude was finally having its way with Gordon, punishing him with waves of nausea and dizziness. His abnormal thirst was unquenched by handfuls of snow. He concentrated on setting a rhythm for himself: *Breathe, step, breathe, step.* Grinding his teeth, he willed one foot before the next over a tricky jumble of erosion-shattered slabs.

At long last Gordon reached the top, which he discovered marked the summit of a massive ridge. It was all bare rock, blown clear of snow. Before him lay the full length of the Sierra crest, a spine of soaring peaks towering up over fourteen thousand feet. The stupendous view had no effect on him. All he could think about were his throbbing feet, the dull pain of his injuries.

Jerry raised his head weakly from the litter. "I wonder how we'd look to a spotter plane."

"I doubt if they could even see us."

Gordon picked his way along the ridge at a disheartened pace. Every rise, every pass and palisade they would have to conquer was visible from here.

A weathered plywood sign was posted on the side of the path:

SKYLINE FIREROAD 14 MI
SYLVAN TRAIL 27 MI
(Compliments of U.S. Forest Service)

He glanced up at Skyline Fireroad. It appeared deceptively closer than ever, an optical illusion that suggested four miles, not fourteen.

After catching his breath, Gordon struggled with the litter down the lee side of the ridge, past a profusion of tufted conifers poking through the snow. It wasn't until he sank waist-deep in the corn snow that he realized they were the tops of trees.

"This just isn't working," he said, gasping for breath.

Gordon was losing his patience with the snow. If it got much deeper, he wouldn't be able to hold out. He was not cut out to be a beast of burden. *How would Howard DeRosa handle this?* he wondered.

Just the way you're doing it, Gordie. You just do the best you can. You've gotta keep on keepin' on.

Jerry moaned and rubbed his hip. "I'm not feeling too hot either." His face had turned gray and waxy. "You'd make faster time without me."

Gordon gripped his shoulder. "I don't want to hear that shit,

Jer. I told you, I'm getting you out of here."

"Then come back for me with the rescue people. You've got to save those kids first."

"*Me* save the kids?" Gordon coughed. "*We're* the ones who need to be saved. We need Del to help us."

Jerry turned his head and vomited into the snow, leaving a steaming bile-green stain. Gordon looked away.

Jerry moaned. "They could be in serious trouble, Gordon," he said after a moment.

"I know. We've talked about that."

"I wouldn't count much on Del."

"What do you mean? He's the only one with the leadership skills to pull them through. If he's not leading them, they *are* in serious trouble."

Jerry rested his head on his arm. "Then why didn't they come back to check on us? That was a big mistake, Gordon."

"They're just kids, Jer. They were scared. And what's that got to do with Del? He's a natural, born leader."

"Is he?" Jerry shook his head. "I don't know, appearances can be deceiving. Del's always so gung ho, he likes to play at being the leader. But when lives are at stake, who knows what he'll do?"

"I'm just not worried about Del," Gordon assured him. But the words belied his feelings; maybe Jerry was right. A seed of doubt had been planted.

"I still say you should go."

Gordon laid a hand on his arm. "Nothing will make me leave you here, Jer. Please get that through your head." He turned away to hide any sign of misgivings. "Let's talk about something else. Like how to get through this goddamned snow."

Gordon dug determinedly into the snow until he unearthed the boughs of a sugar pine. With his knife he cut away six boughs and stripped lengths of resiny bark from the trunk.

"What are you doing?" Jerry asked.

"Building footgear." He fashioned the bark into impromptu shoelaces and strapped the boughs to his boots.

Giving them a cursory test, he set off with Jerry in tow, dragging the sled in a clumsy, splayed-leg gait.

"Looks like we're in business," Gordon said.

They passed a stand of firs whose trunks were all uniformly snapped off at mid-girth, twenty feet above the snow.

"Must have been an avalanche here last winter," Gordon commented, stopping again to catch his breath. "Gives you a good idea of how much snow there is around here in February."

Jerry grunted. He had fallen halfway off his litter, an arm trailing behind in the snow. Gordon stopped and pulled him back into position.

Whump.

Something had fallen in the snow behind them like a heavy footfall. Gordon whipped around, but saw only the unbroken monotony of the snowfield, the silent crags. What had made that sound? The fear of not knowing was more unnerving than any telltale sign of danger.

"I need a rest," he told Jerry. "I must be further gone than I thought." There was no reply.

I'm not surprised that an iggerant washout like you can't make the grade, sonny boy. Now you take this wet-mop, y'hear? I want to see this boiler room as clean as a whistle.

A new panic gripped Gordon: Where were the matches? He checked his breast pocket. They were still there, and he scolded himself for forgetting. Hadn't he just checked them minutes ago? Was he losing his marbles?

The thought of going mad in The Wilds triggered an immediate rush of adrenaline.

Whump.

The sound had come from dead ahead this time, directly in his line of vision—yet invisible. What was it? An aural *fata morgana*? No, he decided, it had to be moving layers of snow, like drifting continental plates. That had to be it.

"Gordon, look!" Jerry said in a loud outburst, startling him. He pointed ahead. "Over there!"

On the next rise there was a crush of footprints in the snow. In the distance rose a hazy brown plume of campfire smoke.

19

Del

Never, never, it never should have happened!

Del grimly bulldozed his way through the knee-deep snowfield, carving a trail for the others. He couldn't take his mind off Lewis. Though he had not known the shy, taciturn boy very well, Del was acutely aware of his absence. One of their number was dead. Del had been the one in charge; he should have somehow prevented it.

Page followed in Del's wake, trying to catch up. "I don't mean to impose, Del. But just to satisfy my curiosity, what happens if we don't make it to Skyline Fireroad by tonight?"

"We'll make it," Del said, trying to sound like a tower of strength.

He increased his stride, pushing himself and the others to their limits. As they struggled to keep up, Del listened to their snow-crunching footsteps resound across the vast stillness of The Wilds like voices over water.

He paused to wait for the others on an exposed granite point. The sky seemed closer at this altitude, a polished blue dome.

Maybe we'll *need the body*, Miles had said. *Like the Donner Party.*

Del had never faced death before. Watching the counselors die had been traumatic enough. But a dead *kid*, that was hitting too close to home.

It could happen to any of us. Your body gets chilled, and you get sleepy, very sleepy. Or you just slip and fall over a ledge.

The others caught up with Del on the point.

"Rest stop," he said, staring dully at his boots.

Everyone slumped to the snow, avoiding each other's eyes. They were on a funeral march without a body. Fear and uneasiness hung over them like the dark, looming shadow of the Sierras.

Miles kicked at the heavy snow in frustration. "We're never going to get anywhere in this shit."

"What we need are snowshoes," Page suggested.

"Good thinking," Del said as an idea struck him. He turned to Haines. "Let me have that hatchet for a minute."

Del walked to a fir and cut away a large square of bark. He found heavy silver duct tape in Gordon's pack and jury-rigged some bindings. "How about that? Snowshoes. We'll make tracks now." He began stripping off a fresh sheet of bark.

Gillian objected. "Isn't that going to kill the tree?"

"That's true," Page agreed. "You're upsetting the ecological balance of nature, Del."

"Are you kidding?" Del said. "You know the story about seven men in a six-man lifeboat?" Gillian and Page shook their heads. "Well, there's a shipwreck, but only six people can fit in the lifeboat. If the seventh one climbs in, the boat'll sink and everyone will drown. So the seventh guy has to be sacrificed so the other six can live. Just think of this pine as that seventh guy. And it's not even a person, it's just a lousy tree."

"So much for Mother Nature," Gillian said.

Del and Kyle helped the little kids cut bark squares while Gillian passed out strips of duct tape. Everyone's mood seemed to lift as they worked. Del was relieved they had something to take their minds off Lewis and his snowy grave.

Within minutes, the snowshoes were finished and the campers gingerly tested out their new footgear.

"Hot damn, they really work!" Miles exclaimed with amazement, taking a bounding step forward. The tip of his snowshoe grazed a drift and he tumbled to the ground.

"Way to go, Miles," Page said. "Thinking with your feet, as usual."

"Stuff it, wiseass."

"You've got to lift each foot clear every time you take a step," Del suggested.

It took the campers a while to perfect the technique of snow-walking. Gordon would have been proud; Del had used his gray matter as survival gear.

A knee-knocking climb over a steep gully led the group into the reaches of a vast, open, gently rising slope. Rock chimneys and rills of snowmelt punctuated the terrain. The jagged heights and defiles of the Sierra crest delimited the upper reaches of the snowfield, towering so high they seemed like the edge of the planet. Below lay a dark scalloped edge of conifers: the timberline.

Not even trees will grow up here, Del mused. The barren snowscape beckoned him, challenged him, and he felt the burden of Lewis's death all the more deeply. He would take the campers across this wilderness, keeping them together and alive. He would beat it somehow.

There was a sharp cry from behind him. At the back of the group, Gillian floundered in the snow, clutching her ankle. By the time Del reached her, Kyle and Haines were already examining her foot.

"What happened?"

"My snowshoe broke," she said with a groan. "I think my ankle's sprained."

"I guess I slipped and knocked her down," Haines admitted.

Del exhaled sharply. "Damnit, Haines."

Gillian's snowshoe was a soggy mess of duct tape and broken bark. Kyle moved to repair it with the roll of tape.

"This is just great," Del said. "We've only got five hours left to meet Sam."

"Don't worry about me." Gillian gave him a flat glance. "I won't slow you down."

"That's not what I meant." Del offered his arm. "Come on."

"I can make it by myself." She looked to Kyle as he finished repairing her snowshoe. "Thanks, Kyle."

"No problem," Kyle said.

Del turned away and struck out across the tundra. The campers followed, Gillian limping.

After an hour's progress, Del halted before a deep impassable gorge that cut them off from the route to Skyline Fireroad.

"What the *hell* is that?" Miles gasped.

Del tried to keep a cool head. "We'll just have to find another way up. If we keep heading east, we might be able to climb higher and loop around it." He turned to the others. "That means we'll probably miss Sam's bus tonight. It just can't be helped."

A heavy silence lingered, everyone staring at Del.

"Look, what can I say?" he continued, on the defensive. "If we had a map, this wouldn't have happened. I'm just doing the best I can here." He scanned their faces. "Anyone have a better idea?"

Wind flayed the granite in a low moan.

"Then let's keep on truckin'," he said, turning uphill.

Kyle suddenly spoke up. "I think we should go back down into the trees." Everyone turned. "I mean, we should loop under the gorge, not over it. The snow won't be as deep down there, so we'll make better time. And there's wood for campfires. Maybe even game."

"Game? How are we going to bring down game?"

A few campers tittered nervously.

"Kyle's got a point, Del," Gillian said, rubbing her ankle. "We could build a big bonfire. A search party might see it."

Del shook his head. "Not if we build it under those trees. No search chopper would ever spot us. But we could build it up here."

"With what?" Miles asked.

"Firewood, of course. We'll just have to haul it up. We'll have the Coleman stove, too."

Most of the campers nodded their agreement. But Kyle had already made up his mind.

"Look, you do what you want," he said, moving away. "I'm going down."

Del took a step toward him. "Don't do it, Kyle. You're forgetting the Wolf Pack. Gordon warned us not to separate. We've got to stick it out together—or someone *else* could die."

Kyle regarded him for a moment, hesitating. "I don't want to die any more than you do, man. I just think you're wrong."

"But everyone agrees with me."

"Yeah? I don't remember you getting elected to tell us what to do."

"Look, *pal*, I'm trying to keep everyone safe and sound here. All you seem to care about is saving your own ass."

Kyle tensed and Del could see he had struck a sensitive chord. "That's just what I intend to do," Kyle said and started picking his way down the slope. After a moment, Haines followed.

"Haines!" Del cried, aghast.

Haines kept walking. "I'm sick of taking shit from you, Del."

"Maybe it does make more sense to go down," Gillian said.

Del swallowed his anger. "Why don't you just go, then?"

Stung, Gillian lifted her head archly. "Fine. I will." She turned away and limped after the two defectors.

Del stared at her receding figure in hurt disbelief.

The late afternoon sun shone brightly but did little to warm The Wilds. Chilled and exhausted, Del and his file of campers stumbled over icy torsions and fissures. Though his legs felt like jelly, Del was determined to make better time than Kyle and the others. Nobody spoke.

As dusk came on, the weak, bloated sun soon vanished into a sea of storm clouds on the horizon. The brewing thunderheads mirrored Del's inner turmoil. Kyle had no business splitting up the Wolf Pack. He was entitled to his own opinion, Del didn't begrudge him that. True, Del hadn't been elected leader, but everyone had wanted him to take charge. And in a life-and-death crisis, there could only be one person making decisions. Kyle had overstepped his bounds, doing whatever he wanted instead of acting for the good of the group. But were he, Haines, and Gillian right? Del felt strangely excluded by their actions, as if he were suddenly the odd man out.

"Hey!" Jennifer cried out, pointing up the mountainside. "What's that?"

Del turned. A few hundred feet overhead, a large feline creature the size of a golden retriever was crouched on a flat outcrop.

"It's a mountain lion, I think," Del said, alarmed.

A few of the little kids cringed back in fright.

"What's it doing?" Jennifer asked. She looked intrigued.

The lion held a small rodent in its jaws, whipping it from side to side.

"Far fucking out," Miles said. "He's strangling it."

"Oh no, he sees us," Marcus warned. "He's gonna come for us."

"Just keep moving," Del said, hurrying ahead. "Come on now, pick up the pace."

As the sun set, protruding boulders cast weird black shadows on the scarlet, sun-flamed snowfield: manic, elongated figures of razor-toothed animals, slavering wolves, starving pioneers with a yen for human flesh. *Don't let your imagination run wild,* Del told himself sternly.

"I'm cold," Lonny whimpered. "When're we going to pitch camp?"

"Soon. We'll build ourselves a nice big bonfire." Del had to keep their spirits up, insure their confidence in him. He couldn't afford any more mistakes. "We'll go just a little farther." He turned to Page, cold and exhausted. "Mind over matter, right, Professor?"

Page hugged himself, shivering. "That theory's wearing pretty thin, I'm afraid."

Miles pushed up alongside Del. "How are we going to build that bonfire, man? It's too late to go downhill for wood."

"We've got the Coleman stove."

"What if we run out of food?" Jennifer fretted.

"Then the Donner Man will get us," Lonny babbled. "Chew our bones. Chomp—"

"Cut it out," Del said. "There's no Donner Man, okay? Nothing like that's going to happen."

The black shadows became gorging leeches, sucking away the last smears of crimson dusk. The darkness pressed in on them with a weight of its own, pelting the campers with a new flurry of windborne snow. Del shivered and zipped up his parka to the collar.

"There's something behind that rock!" Lissa cried suddenly, pointing ahead.

"It's *him!*" Lonny screeched.

"Come on, guys," Del said. "There's nothing out here."

"Yeah, button it, you little rug-rat," Miles hissed. "You're seeing things." He turned to the others. "Lonny's going looney on us."

"Actually, there *is* something out there," Page said. "Look."

Del followed Page's finger to a flickering beacon of yellow light some distance ahead, below the timberline.

"Maybe it's the rescue people," Jennifer said.

"No," Del said tightly. "It's just the others."

Miles turned to him, glaring. "Yeah. And they've got a *campfire.*"

The glow danced and capered through the trees, beckoning them.

20

Kyle

The three campers sat around a blazing fire on a dry tarp, wolfing down canned spaghetti and Spam. They had bivouacked a quarter of a mile's trek below the timberline near a running brook. On Kyle's suggestion, they had built their campfire on the stump of a fallen conifer. The stump was ablaze now and would probably burn through the night.

"Bet we make it to the fireroad by noon," Gillian said, sharing a hopeful glance with Haines.

"I hope so." Kyle stared up at the barren, moonlit snowfield. It felt strange to be alone, just the three of them. "Wonder how they're making out up there." He was secretly delighted that Gillian had come with him. *I'm glad you finally stood up to Del*, he wanted to tell her.

"Del's acting like such a child," Gillian said, shaking her head. "All this follow-the-leader crap. No wonder the little kids stick with him. He's one of them."

"I'm surprised *you* didn't stick with him. I thought you two were an item."

Gillian frowned. "I'm not just 'Del's girl,' you know. Just because he was my boyfriend doesn't mean I have to commit suicide with him."

"What if we don't find the fireroad?" Haines asked as he split a piece of firewood with the hatchet. "How long can we hang on?"

"Hard to say." Kyle scratched the snow-reflected sunburn under his chin. "Gordon told us never to underestimate The Wilds. I'm just worried about our food supply. Don't forget we have to hang the food packs up in the trees tonight, by the way."

"How come?" Haines asked.

"The bears, remember?"

"How much food is left?" Gillian said.

"Enough for tomorrow. Maybe for two days if we ration it. After that, except for trail mix and candy, we're on our own. We may have to learn how to hunt."

The others peered at him expectantly.

"Don't ask *me* how to do it," he added with an edge of exasperation. "I'm no expert."

Kyle pondered the irony of his sudden leadership by default. He didn't want people depending on him, had never wanted to lead anyone. He didn't even trust himself—how could he take care of other kids? Leadership meant pressure to perform, and he wasn't about to undertake all that responsibility just to live up to his father's expectations.

Gillian cocked her head, alerted to a sound from the woods. "What was that? Did you hear something?"

"Probably just a squirrel," Kyle said. "I—"

Tramping footsteps cut him short. All three campers jumped to their feet in unison.

Page emerged into the firelight followed by Miles, Jennifer, and the other children, everyone exhausted and shivering from cold. Del trailed in after them, his face chalky and tight-lipped. He looked like he had aged ten years.

Page stopped short of the fire circle, uncertain, then joked, "Don't bother to get up. It's just us saddlebusters home from the range."

"Have some grub," Kyle said, his voice unnaturally loud. "Guess there's enough here for everyone."

Miles and the others scurried in and huddled around the fire, in desperate need of warmth. Del held back; like a leery animal, he steered clear of the fire.

"Hey, what *happened* to you guys?" Haines mocked. "Lose your way or something?"

Del shuffled toward Kyle. "Can we stay here tonight?" he mumbled.

"Sure. Wherever you want, Del."

Only Page made a move for the food. He loaded his tin plate with Spam and scarfed it down. "Mmm ... tastes like horsemeat, but I'm hungry enough to eat a horse." He limped about, mimicking King Richard III. "Horsemeat! Horsemeat! My kingdom for some horsemeat!"

Miles sounded his *baa*-like laugh and hurried in for his share. The little kids rushed to join him. The tension was broken.

After everyone else had helped themselves, Del scooped the last of the spaghetti onto his plate and tried to eat, but had no appetite. His hands were so jittery that his fork clattered against the plate. Everyone else talked among themselves and tried not to look at him.

"It was so fucking cold up there, I thought my buns would freeze and fall off," Miles commented, cleaning his plate.

"You should've come with us," Haines said.

"Can I have seconds, please?" Jennifer asked.

Gillian shook her head. "Sorry, that's it. We've got to ration the food now."

While the kids chatted about the different routes they had taken, Kyle sat down next to Del. Hunched over his plate, Del wouldn't look him in the eye, as though ashamed of his defeat. He smelled terrible.

Kyle fidgeted with a smoldering twig from the fire. "More clouds moving in," he noted. "Could be another storm."

Del grunted. Shoving aside his unfinished plate, he began picking at the filthy dressing on his cheek, where a spate of acne had broken out. A puffy blue bruise showed through.

"You shouldn't touch that," Kyle advised.

"It itches."

Jennifer came over and stared at Del's untouched food with the look of a baby vulture. "Can I have that?"

Del nodded, still averting his eyes from Kyle.

"Look, it's my fault," Kyle said finally. "I tried to tell you that on the Dragonback."

"What is?" Del asked with a vacant look.

"That." Kyle gestured at Del's cheek. "I made you fall. I was pissed because I'd fucked up and you wouldn't let me carry the flag."

"Who cares now?" Del said, rising wearily. "I'm going to sleep, so watch the fire, okay? Make sure it doesn't die on us."

Del stumbled off and unfurled his sleeping bag on a tarp, not even bothering to set up his tent. He fell asleep almost instantly.

Kyle plodded down to a stream bank where the others were washing up from dinner.

"What did he say?" Gillian asked, rinsing her plate.

Kyle hesitated. "He thinks it might snow some more."

"That's a real pearl of wisdom," Page snorted. "All you have to do is look up."

Kyle picked up a scrub pad and bent down to the water's edge, but lost his footing on the icy bank and started to slide. Gillian managed to grab the back of his parka, breaking his fall, then lost her own footing and plunged feet first into the brook. With a yelp, she bolted up in the freezing waist-high water and scrambled onto the bank. Kyle rushed to her.

"I'm okay," she blurted, already shivering violently.

"Haines, help me here! Let's get those wet clothes off her, quick."

The two hustled her back to camp. Inside Kyle's tent they peeled off her soaking boots and socks.

"I'm okay," Gillian insisted over and over.

Dazed and shaking, she struggled unsuccessfully to get her sweater off. The other children crowded around the open tent flap.

Kyle waved them away. "Go heat up some water," he told them. "Haines, you unroll her sleeping bag while I get this wet stuff off her."

He would have to peel off her pants, an intimidating thought. He'd never hear the end of it from the others. But there was no time to lose. He hastily untied her belt and eased the jeans off over the swell of her hips.

"Put the blanket over me," Gillian said with chattering teeth.

Her legs were gray and felt like refrigerated rubber. Kyle rubbed them with all the vigor he could muster.

21

Del

Del awoke from a nap so profound that, for a foggy moment, he could not remember where he was. Lifting his head, he looked out into the night and saw movement through the open flap of Kyle's tent. There was a half-naked girl in there. *Gillian?* Kyle was massaging her legs.

Del watched for a long time, fascinated by the steady handiwork on her passive, prone body. *She could at least show some resistance.* Del's ears began to ring, his pulse throbbing loudly in his temples. He bolted to his feet and fled crazily into the woods. Towering firs reared up before him, blurring through his tears.

I knew it! I goddamned knew it!

An icy nimbus of wind dried his eyes. The pain and hurt slowly percolated into anger. He had befriended Kyle, brought him out of his shell, helped him find acceptance at camp: Kyle was *Del Albright's buddy*, he was okay. Was this Kyle's way of saying thanks, blood brother?

Del turned to a foxtail pine and gave it a savage kick. A load of snow dumped over him. He pummeled the tree in despair.

The wind picked up into a steady gale, blowing whorls of spindrift into his face. Then it began to snow, large hail-shaped particles pelting the ground.

"Harder!" he urged, baring his face to the snowfall. "Keep it coming!"

He wanted a real blizzard, a cataclysm that would bury the two of them in their tent

"Come on," he cried to the storm. *"Show your teeth!"*

22

Gordon

"I'd better count our matches." Gordon feverishly unzipped the pocket of his parka. "Just to be sure."

"By all means," Jerry croaked.

The two men were huddled over a flickering fire in a cave Gordon had discovered before nightfall. A blizzard raged outside. Gusts of air found their way into the cave, fanning the fire.

"This blow's going to burn up all our wood," Gordon fretted, feeding another branch into the flames.

"Uh-huh."

Jerry was propped up against the cavern wall. His face was flushed, a false rosiness brought on by the fever. Gordon had to admire him for toughing it out as well as he had.

"How're you doing over there?" Gordon asked, setting some water to boil in the tin cup. Jerry did not answer. "It's midnight snack time. I highly recommend the chunky beef soup with rice for starters, but the maître d' tells me we just ran out. So you must try today's blue-plate special: boiled trail mix *aux fines herbes.*"

Jerry just stared at him, unblinking, a man who knew his time was running out. "I didn't like you, Gordon. Not at first."

Gordon looked up, not really surprised. "I suppose they told you about Cal Wolcroft."

"I read your file. I knew you'd been fired from the teaching job. But the Gulch's owners hired you back because you knew the camp. And The Wilds, of course. No one else was available."

"You mean no one else would come," Gordon said. "I was probably their only choice, the desperate buggers." He laughed and rubbed his eyes. "You had no idea what you were getting into up here, did you, Jer? I *tried* to warn you about the weather. I *told* you the Ordeal wasn't going to be some Mickey Mouse stroll through the park." Gordon softened his tone. "You were a greenhorn."

"You're right, I guess I was a greenhorn." Jerry tried to sit up but could not. He rested his head against the stony wall. "But we've gotten past that, you and I."

Gordon nodded, his throat tightening. "Yes, we have," he said in a muffled voice.

"Cal Wolcroft." Jerry sighed. "Awful thing to have happen, Gordie."

"Tell me about it."

"I never wanted to bring it up. It must be tough for you."

"Yeah, it is."

"You'd think they'd want to annihilate every mountain lion in the county after something like that."

Gordon tilted his head. "What mountain lion?" he said with an unblinking gaze. "I never heard about any mountain lion."

"There was an autopsy on the Wolcroft boy, that's what I was told. The teeth marks came from a mountain lion. The county sent in a team of hunters with rifles to track it down. They never found it."

"No one told me," Gordon said, his voice a dry whistle. "It was the end of the summer."

"I'm amazed they didn't."

A mountain lion! Gordon felt a wave of relief. For a moment he wanted to cheer, dance a jig. Then the anger hit him.

"They could have at least *told* me. Even a postcard! God, I could use a drink now."

Jerry coughed, his face paler than before. "Me, I'd like some of that chunky beef soup with rice." He averted his head and heaved violently. Then he rolled on his back, immobile.

"Jerry? You okay?"

Fearing the worst, Gordon scrambled to his side. Jerry's breathing was deep and regular; he had simply fallen asleep.

Gordon wiped his mouth and pulled the sleeping bag up around his throat.

The wind settled down to a low lull and Gordon poked his head outside. The blizzard had finished its business. Dull melon-colored moonlight drooled down through the filmy cloud cover. In a gap of black, cloudless sky, a winking mote of light caught Gordon's eye. It was probably a commercial flight. The people inside the plane took it for granted that they were warm and dry. They were drinking wine and working their way through a choice of chicken Kiev or lasagna with chocolate mousse for dessert. In first class, there was free champagne and the in-flight movie had started. None of the passengers knew they were flying over a haunted wilderness, a white hell that held two battered counselors and twelve campers trapped in its clutches.

Jerry wrenched out a sharp cry, startling Gordon from his thoughts.

"Jerry?"

The black, demonic wind began to groan, gathering momentum again.

"You okay?" Gordon said.

Jerry's eyes were wide open, the pupils rolled back into his head. Gordon gripped his wrist. There was no pulse. The wind groaned insistently.

Staggering to his feet, Gordon threw himself at the cave opening. He screamed back at The Wilds in a rising howl of anguish.

23

Kyle

Unable to sleep, Kyle rose at daybreak and emerged from his tent into a thick, claustrophobic bank of fog. He was the only one awake. The storm was over, the snow as grim and colorless as porridge. The fire on the charred tree stump had gone out

A high insectile buzz broke the morning stillness. It sounded at first like a fly, then a model airplane. The noise grew into the throaty pounding of a helicopter. Kyle craned his neck until he saw it: a fog-enshrouded chopper sweeping in low over the treetops with a deafening roar. It passed almost directly overhead.

Campers began moving inside their tents. Gillian was the first one out. She seemed fully recovered from her fall and her dousing in the creek

"Did you see it?" she asked, excited.

"Yeah, I saw it."

Del crawled out from under a tarp, dirty and bleary-eyed. "Where is it? Did they see us?"

Kyle shook his head.

As the rest of the campers crawled outside, the metallic whine slowly faded until silence closed back in on them.

Del turned on Kyle, his eyes burning like studs of ice. "You … you let the signal fire go out! We could've been rescued, don't you realize that?"

"Bullshit, man," Kyle countered. "They could never see us in this fog unless we lit up the whole frigging mountain."

"Jesus, Kyle! Am I the only one here who cares about how

we get out of this mess?" Del grabbed a rock and hurled it into the embers. "If it weren't for *you*, we wouldn't be here in the first place. Gordon and Mr. Dugan, even Lewis would still be alive!"

At a loss for words, Kyle stood rooted to the ground.

"I can't believe you said that," Gillian said, shocked.

"Del's right," said Miles, moving to his side. "We should've built a fire above the timberline. We might be stuck here for days now."

"Weeks," Lonny chimed in. "Forever!"

"I think we're overreacting here," Page said.

"Take back what you said, Del," Gillian insisted. "Right now."

Del ignored her. "Strike camp, everybody," he shouted to the rest. "We've got to get uphill and start a fire, fast. You guys who stay behind better *pray* that chopper comes back."

"Come on, Del," Frank said, exasperated. "So we let the fire go out, that's not a felony. I say we stay here—*together*. Remember what happened yesterday."

"Why don't we build two fires?" Page suggested. "One above the timberline, one down here."

Del shook his head. "I think it's a little late for that." He jammed his gear into his pack. Miles and a few small kids followed suit, but many more held back, unsure. They looked to Kyle to say something.

"That's the problem here, Del." Kyle's voice was dead calm. "No one's supposed to have any opinion but you. You've made just as many mistakes as any of us. And you said it yourself: We stand a better chance if we stick together."

"Let him go, Kyle," Gillian said, turning to Del. "Go *on*, why don't you. But if you screw things up again, don't come crawling back to us."

Del glared at her bitterly. "Look who's talking. You're screwing up as much as you're *screwing around*."

"What's that supposed to mean?" Gillian demanded.

"Hey, let's cool it," Kyle said, intervening.

Del turned to the others. "Anyone who stays down here doesn't stand a chance in hell. Miles, Frank, let's get a move on. You too, Haines."

"I'll take my chances with Kyle," Haines said. He faced Del. "Have a nice day, asshole."

"I'm staying put, too," Frank said.

Del stiffened. "Just wait until the rescue choppers come. Maybe we won't even *tell* them about you brain-damaged jerks down here."

"Yeah, if you're not dead already—thanks to Kyle," Miles piped in. "You'd be better off with the Donner Man for a leader."

Kyle tried to contain his fury. "Are you guys listening to yourselves? You sound about eight years old." He raised his hands in a conciliatory gesture. "Look, why don't we just cool down a minute and talk this thing out."

"Cool down?" Del exploded. "*Cool down?*" Look at you—you're no leader! You don't even *want* to be a leader. You can't be depended on, you screw everything up, you let people *die*! You even let your own brother drown, didn't you? *Didn't you!*"

With a snarl of rage, Kyle suddenly sprang at Del. They toppled to the snow. Kyle wrestled Del onto his back in a blind rush of fury, trying to pin him down.

"Don't you ever," he screamed, "*ever* say that again!" He grabbed hold of Del's hood and slammed his head to the snow.

Del scissor-kicked, easily tossing Kyle off to one side. Kyle rolled and slammed against a boulder, winded.

"You dumb shit," Del growled, jumping to his feet as though he had disposed of a pesky insect. He marched over to Gordon's pack and helped himself to matches and supplies. "I'm only taking our fair share."

"This comes with us," said Miles, hefting the firewood hatchet. "We wouldn't want Kyle to use it on somebody, would we?" He directed his words toward the little kids. "He might get hungry and turn one of you small fries into a Donner Man Special."

"Jesus." Gillian turned away in disgust.

"Yeah, really, Miles," Page said. "That's a little childish, don't you think?"

But Miles's words had hit home with Lonny and the younger ones. Kyle could see it in their eyes as he lay puffing in the snow.

"You coming?" Del asked them.

Except for Page, the small campers collected their gear and quickly followed Del and Miles uphill toward the timberline.

24

Gordon

Without a shovel, Gordon could not break through ice and snow to dig a proper grave. He finally gave up and left Jerry's body inside the cave, doing his best to block the entrance with rocks to ward off predators.

"I'll find those campers, Jer. I swear I will."

Get real. All you want to do is save your own butt.

Slumping on a flat boulder, Gordon forced himself to eat the rest of the trail mix. His injuries were more painful today, his muscles tight and sore. He knew he had limited endurance, and time was running out. He needed energy and brainpower to reassess his predicament.

Gordon scanned the terrain. Snow hung over the tops of the passes and upthrust ridges, resembling torn veils. Beyond lay a thick fog bank. The campers, he suspected, were somewhere in that pea soup. Chances were that no rescue team would find them under these conditions. That meant a reprieve for Gordon, another day to catch up.

Gordon consulted his topographic map. Ahead stretched a gentle, sloping snowfield. The kids had no map, he reasoned; they were probably bushwhacking their way toward the Skyline Fireroad on the path of least resistance, a circuitous route at best. But they could never cross Devil's Dropoff, a steep-walled chasm lying directly in their path. They would be forced to detour some other way.

On his map, Gordon noticed a steep path that cut over a high choppy ridge to the north. If he could climb it, he would shortcut five miles off his trek and possibly come down *in front* of the campers. There would be hot food, sleeping bags, tents, equipment. God, what a lovely thought. He had almost forgotten that such creature comforts existed. Together they would build a huge smoky signal fire. The rescue team would call him a hero. His story would make the front page of *The New York Times.*

The jagged ridge was only five hundred feet up, but the grade seemed impossibly steep and there was no switchback trail to help him. Gordon fashioned a four-foot snow-stabber from a sapling and started up the incline. He was lucky: The snow had crusted over, allowing him to punch in footholds with his toes, using the snow-stabber for leverage. Inuring himself to the pain, he kept his belly in and his back taut, his center of gravity close to the slope.

If I only had crampons, this mother would be a piece of cake.

The sun began to shine through a break in the fog and reflected harshly off the snow, nearly blinding him. His breath came in fiery heaves. Salty sweat dripped into his wounds.

Breathe. Kick. Hold. Breathe. Kick. Hold.

He could not go on, but he had to. The blisters on his feet and ankles pulsed with each uphill step. Pain and exertion held sway over darker thoughts: Jerry, the campers, the hopelessness of it all. He glanced down over his shoulder, surprised by the distance he had climbed. Yet, as he looked up, the top of the ridge seemed no closer than before.

Stop. You need to catch your breath.

—No I don't.

Loose scree began shifting under the snow, and Gordon slid back six inches for every foot gained, as if climbing a down escalator. He rested for a spell, clinging to the snowy incline, his mouth rasping against the ice. It wouldn't take more than a wiggle for the mountain to flick him away like an annoying flea.

Gordon tried to kick another step into the incline, but his right leg wouldn't budge. It tingled with prickly sleep. There was no feeling at all in the foot.

Paralyzed, Gordon imagined his death. He would be a frozen corpse clinging forever to a corrugated cliff, never to be found or buried. He would become a part of The Wilds, as permanent as a wax figure in a museum, haunting hapless climbers as The Wilds had haunted him.

25

Kyle

The black rabbit sensed their presence at twenty feet. It darted toward the creek bed in a flurry of snow.

"Let's track it," Kyle whispered to Haines, a gray human shape in the fog behind him.

They both carried spears fashioned from hunting knives taped to sticks of wood. Kyle was determined to prove they could bring down game, survive in The Wilds—and do it better than Del.

You even let your own brother drown, didn't you!

Those terrible words kept worming their way back into Kyle's thoughts. How could Del possibly know? *Nobody* knew the truth but Marshall. But it was the intent behind the words that hurt the most. Del had gone too far, destroyed something between them forever. There could be no reconciliation or forgiveness between them now.

For the brief time they had been friends, Del was the big brother Kyle had always wanted Marshall to be. Kyle would have liked growing up with someone like Del, a stable rock of support, a buddy instead of an autistic wild child. They could have shared summer jobs together, played on the same teams together, partied together. They would have made a formidable pair.

"Got it!" Haines shouted. He pounced, just grazing the rabbit with outstretched hands.

Kyle saw his chance and dove. He cornered the animal against a granite outcrop and grabbed it by the scruff of the neck. The spear went high over his head, ready for the kill.

"Nice going!" Haines whooped.

The rabbit flailed frantically in Kyle's grip, begging for freedom with liquid eyes. A rivulet of urine squirted onto the snow. Kyle hesitated, then, almost apologetically, released the animal.

"What the ..." Haines stared at Kyle, perplexed.

The rabbit lay on its side for an instant, then bounded out of sight.

Kyle slumped to the snow. "I wanted to, but ..."

"Yeah, I know. I couldn't have done it either."

26

Gordon

Gordon had reached the summit. He lay panting atop the ridge for a small eternity, gazing skyward and panting, his mind as blank as the walls of the drifted parapets that surrounded him.

He shielded his eyes from the beam of sunlight bearing down on him, harsh as a spotlight. The rest of the mountain had returned to shadow. He could feel gusts of wind tugging at him, the cold seeping through his parka. But beyond the registering of sensations, his brain refused to function. Everything merged with featureless uniformity. Then he noticed a dragonfly lying next to him in the snow. It was dead, yet outlined by a strange rainbowlike aura, each band of color a myriad of glowing dots. He touched the insect's wings, and the aura spread to his hand, ringing it with all the colors of the spectrum.

This must be snowblindness, Gordon thought. He remembered reading about it.

"Overexposure to sunlight without glacier glasses will result in visual distortions, or even a temporary loss of vision," he intoned, as if reading from a textbook. If he went blind now, he would surely perish.

Onward and upward.

With herculean effort, Gordon rose and stumbled to the edge of the summit. He peered into the fog bank hanging over the timberline. The campers had to be down there somewhere.

He started slowly down the rocky slope, coping with slippery footing all the way, until he came to an impassable drop-off, a sheer vertical wall that shot down for hundreds of feet. Gordon stared at it uncomprehendingly, confused and frightened, then fumbled for his topo map. No, he hadn't made a mistake. The mountain had somehow changed. An avalanche or erosion must have set off a major slide, peeling away a giant chunk of granite. The climb had been a wasted effort; he would have to go back up and then down the way he had come. He cursed The Wilds for its treachery.

Halfway back down the other side, Gordon heard what sounded like a gunshot somewhere uphill. Near the summit, a tiny rock was bouncing down the incline. It hit a patch of ice and skidded faster, now the size of a soccer ball. Gordon studied its swift progress toward him, transfixed. The projectile plowed through a fragile drift—big as a melon—and whizzed past Gordon's face. Strangely he had felt no fear, only mild curiosity. His reflexes, even his train of thought, seemed to be slowing down. That could be deadly in terrain like this. He turned and continued downhill, clinging to the mountainside.

On the final stretch, a foothold gave way. Gordon slid, whooshing downhill like a runaway sled, the wind roaring in his ears. It was exhilarating, almost fun. At the bottom, dots of red fabric caught his eye. Gordon dug his hands into the snow pack, braking to a halt.

Shreds of Jerry's parka festooned the jumble of rocks that had been dug away from the mouth of the cave. A few freshly picked bones, clean and pinkish-white, were scattered on the snow crust. The rest of the body had been dragged away.

The contents of Gordon's stomach gushed into his throat, choking off a scream. He wanted to run, flee, escape. It was Cal Wolcroft all over again. A wave of dry heaves racked him. When it had passed, he gathered up the remains in the torn parka. Should he bury them again?

Keep the bones, whispered the voice of mad reason. They were full of protein-rich marrow. *It would be a pity to let them go to waste, don't you think?*

Revolted, Gordon covered his face with his gloves.

A pity … yes, a great pity.

That must have been the way the Donner Party had seen it. *Chow down, you party animal,* Gordon thought, giggling hoarsely to himself. His lunatic laugh rose, echoing over the white wilderness.

27

Del

"I'm king of the mountain!"

Del stood high atop a rounded hummock, proud and lordlike. Snow-cradled peaks surrounded him, glowing brightly in the late afternoon sun. Far below, the timberline remained hidden by thick gray fog.

"Come, you peasants!" he shouted to his pack as they circled the hummock. "I dare you to dethrone your king!"

"Let's get him, knights!" Miles bellowed. "May the Force be with us!" He led a circular assault that Del easily fended off with thrusts of his boots.

Earlier, after leaving Kyle's camp, Del had led his party high up the mountain and made camp in a hollow between two boulders. He had built a roaring signal fire from wood collected on the way. If any more rescue helicopters flew by, Del's beacon would burn bright enough for anyone to see. He still toyed with the notion of leaving Kyle's party to rot in The Wilds; they certainly deserved it. He wouldn't do it, of course, but he *could* if he wanted to. He had the power; the might of right would be on his side.

"Back, you barbarians!" Del yelled, lightly shoving Miles away from the hummock. "Off my kingdom!"

A long, plaintive howl rose up in the distance, startling everyone. It echoed eerily off the snow-clad planes of granite, a tortured, almost human cry that made Del shiver.

"Wolf," Lonny croaked, stiffening in terror. "Wolf," he sobbed, "wolf."

Miles rolled his eyes. "Shut up, Looney."

"There aren't any wolves in the Sierras," Del said, descending from his throne. "Mr. Dugan said so."

"If it wasn't a wolf, then what was it?" Jennifer asked.

Del hesitated. "Probably a coyote."

He hoped he sounded more convincing than he felt. *There* is *something else up here besides us.* Something primordial. He had known that since the first day of the Ordeal in the enchanted woods.

The little ones smiled, reassured. They believed in him. Like the sorcerer's apprentice, they would follow him anywhere.

The fire was burning down, their wood reserve dwindling. The Coleman stove had run out of fuel.

"Okay, guys, it's time to play the Firewood Game," Del announced. "The signal fire is hungry. It wants us to feed it."

"Firefood!" Lissa exclaimed.

"Exactly. This will be our special game. No one else can play."

Del held out his arms to embrace The Wilds. "We're *all* kings of the mountain up here. And we'll have so much fun we won't … we won't even mind if it takes a little longer to get rescued." He had almost said *we won't ever want to go back.* "So let's make the signal fire happy, okay? And for every kid who brings back an armful of firewood, there'll be a big piece of chocolate."

"Firefood! Firefood!" rang a chorus of voices.

"But I already brought wood up before," Jennifer declared with a no-nonsense scowl. "I want my chocolate *now.*"

Del shook his head. "Listen up, everyone," he warned. "The Firewood Game isn't all fun and games. There are obstacles, dangers, just like in Dungeons and Dragons."

"What kind of dangers?" Lonny asked.

"The Donner Man, of course," Miles said. "He might catch you and eat you alive. Or he might push you off a cliff, like he did to Gordon and Mr. Dugan. Or kill you in a snow cave like you-know-who." He gestured down toward the timberline. "So whatever you do, don't go near the Donner Man's camp."

"That's enough, Miles." Del shot him a reprimanding look. "Just cool it."

"Kyle's not the Donner Man," Jennifer objected.

Del sensed a wave of uneasiness run through the kids, and it worried him. "Let's go, let's go," he cried, clapping his hands like a schoolteacher. "Time's a'wasting. Come on troops, one foot in front of the other now."

28

Kyle

Dusk fell, the mist darkening to deeper shades of gray.
Kyle and his small band sat around the firepit in silence.
Unwashed, hungry, and disconsolate, they consumed their last
civilized meal from the packs: macaroni and cheese.

"How many matches did Del leave us?" Page asked.

"Just a dozen," Kyle said.

"I've *had* it with Del," Haines grumbled. "He's always acting
so fucking high and mighty, then he comes limping in here with
his tail between his legs, begging us for food. Next thing you
know, he's trying to boss us around all over again."

"How're we going to manage without the hatchet?" Page
wondered. He was the only little kid who hadn't followed Del
back up the mountain.

"I don't know," Kyle said. "Getting firewood is going to be a
bitch. We'll have to make do with junk wood."

"No big deal," Gillian said. "Better that than having to put
up with Del. Let him keep the stupid thing, as long as he stays
out of our way."

"He had no *right* to take it," Frank grumbled.

"Hey, we don't have any monopoly on the hatchet," Kyle
said. "There are twice as many of them as there are of us
anyway. We'll get by without it."

He climbed down to the creek to wash his plate. In the
dying light he noticed wildflowers peeking out of the snowy
bank, little miracles of color.

Gillian joined him, toting the macaroni pot.

"Look," he said, pointing.

"They're beautiful! Like that poppy field in *The Wizard of Oz.*"

"See that one over there? Western azalea. And that's mustang clover. Those are crimson columbine, I think."

"Did you learn all that from a *National Geographic* special too?" she asked with a smile.

"No, my old man's a gardening freak. He's really into the exotic stuff. Guess it just rubbed off."

"Come on, let's pick some," Gillian said, leading him by the hand to the bank.

"What for?"

"I don't know. Does there have to be a reason?"

"I guess not. It's just that Dad never picked them. He said they were part of nature and shouldn't be disturbed."

"Yeah, that's what the Sierra Club says too." Gillian seemed tempted to pick them anyway. She glanced at Kyle. "How old were you when your parents got divorced?"

"Twelve. You?"

"Ten. I never knew what was going on with Mom and Daddy. They never fought, they were always so civilized and proper—the model suburban family. But they walked around with brown clouds over their heads most of the time. I always thought they were mad at me for something."

Kyle nodded. "I know the feeling. My dad *is* always mad at me."

Gillian dipped the macaroni pot in the creek. "Really. So when they finally split up, it was a total surprise. It felt like they were divorcing *me.*"

"You didn't have any brothers or sisters?"

"Nope, I'm an only child. That just made it harder."

"I went through the same kind of shit," Kyle said. "My old man was never satisfied with anything I did. It's like he kept this chalkboard in the sky, a list of all the ways I let him down. He'd bring up how much he was disappointed because I didn't give a rat's ass about Little League. Or how angry he felt about the time I didn't want to help him jack up the car on cinder blocks and tinker with the stupid carburetor. I was supposed to like all the things he liked. On top of that, I had an autistic brother to look after, which just made things worse."

"The one who died, right?"

Kyle nodded, tight-lipped.

"Is it true, you know, what Del said about him?"

"What do you mean?"

"Something about him drowning …"

"I don't want to talk about it."

"Hey!" Haines called out, ambling down from the campsite with a smirk on his face. "What are you guys up to? Dickin' each other in the daisy patch?"

"Grow up," Gillian said, rinsing the pot.

The others joined them on the bank, ending the conversation. Relieved, Kyle started back uphill. The truth about Marshall was better left unsaid. He didn't want to start what he wasn't willing to finish.

When the group arrived back at camp, the fire was dead and smoking.

"Holy shit," Frank muttered.

"What happened?" Gillian asked, looking angrily at the others. "Who put it out?"

"We didn't do it, we were out getting firewood," Haines said. "Must have been Del and those guys."

Gillian turned livid. "Those assholes. We should organize a raiding party and give them a little of their own medicine."

"Yeah," Haines agreed. "That scumbag should get what's coming to him."

Kyle shook his head. "Forget it."

"Why should we?" Gillian stared at him, surprised. "We can't just take this lying down."

"Gil, we don't know what happened. We can't just blame everything on Del."

"Why do you keep standing up for that jerk?"

"That 'jerk' used to be your boyfriend, remember?"

"But who *else* could've done it?" Haines asked. "The Donner Man, I suppose?" He leaned against a sugar pine and a load of snow dumped onto his head.

Everyone laughed but Kyle. "Look at that branch," he said, pointing to the sugar pine that leaned over the fire. "No snow on it. Chances are the heat of the fire loosened the snow. It must have fallen off and doused the fire. See? Blame it on nature, not on Del." He knelt down and started laying wood for a new blaze.

"Sounds logical," Page said in a clinical tone, trying to sound like Mr. Spock. "Gravitationally speaking, his theory is congruent with the physical data."

Haines shrugged. "Yeah, well. I still wouldn't put it past Del."

"Maybe, maybe not," Gillian said, still unsure. She squatted by the fire to help Kyle pile up new kindling and tinder.

Kyle glanced at her. "Maybe, maybe not," he teased, giving her a wry smile.

She smiled, her face softening. The smile gave Kyle a fresh sense of confidence and confirmed a growing realization: He was the leader of this expedition.

29

Del

Del's signal fire burned weakly under a light but unrelenting snowfall. The wood supply was dwindling fast.

"I want to go home," Lonny wailed. "I'm cold."

"I'm hungry," Jennifer bellowed.

"My stomach hurts," Lissa cried.

Del dashed from child to child, reassuring each that everything would be okay. But his frazzled patience was running out. As the last streaks of daylight faded, the camp was turning into a bedlam of whining, mewling children.

Miles sat glumly on a tarp, methodically throwing the hatchet into a firewood branch and wrenching it out, over and over. He watched Del trying to cope with the younger ones, not lifting a finger to help.

Candy wrappers and refuse littered the snow. "This place is a pigsty, let's clean it up," Del had told the kids earlier. They had paid no attention to him.

"We better not go to sleep tonight," Jennifer warned the others. "The Donner Man'll get us in our dreams. Just like Freddy Kreuger."

"Who?" Lissa asked.

"You know, from *A Nightmare on Elm Street.*"

The others nodded solemnly.

"I know one way to keep the Donner Man away," Jennifer went on. "Rub pine sap and dirt all over ourselves. Then we'll taste too icky to eat."

"Watch out, guys," Miles cackled, tossing the hatchet. "Freddy's *back*!"

"Come on, everybody," Del said, "we're all going down to play the Firewood Game again."

"I don't want to play." Lonny peered down at the blotchy timberline. "He's down there, he's waiting to get us."

"Who is? Kyle?"

"No. You know … *him*."

Del turned to Miles, exasperated. "Come on, Miles, I could use a little assistance here."

Miles merely rolled his eyes and continued his hatchet-throwing game.

"Thanks for nothing," Del said.

He turned to the little kids. "Look, I know it seems scary down there, but unless we feed the signal fire, the choppers can't come and rescue us. Understand?"

"I am *hungry*," Jennifer insisted with a determined scowl.

"I know, I know. Just as soon as you bring up your share of firewood, you'll get your piece of choco—"

"No! *I want it now!*"

"Me too!" Lonny cried. "Feed me! Feed *me!*"

The others spontaneously took up the chant: *"Feed me! Feed me!"*

"Okay, okay." Del handed the remaining chocolate bar to Jennifer, expecting her to dole it out to the others. She stuffed the entire bar into her mouth. "No, you're supposed to share it."

"Unfair, unfair!" Lonny screamed.

"Just for that," Marcus said, "we're going to cut her up and eat her."

"Unless I eat you first," she retorted through her full mouth. Marcus reeled back, surprised by her ferocity.

"Come on, Del," Miles urged. "Give the suckers the rest of the goddamn chocolate. You'll never get them moving at this rate."

Del shook his head. "That was it."

Miles's eyes widened. "Are you shitting me?"

"I told you, if we'd rationed it, we would've had enough for two days."

"Hey, blood, you're the one in charge. You blew it."

"I don't see *you* doing anything to help, Miles."

"I'm getting real sick of this shit." Miles kept on throwing the hatchet and Del finally yanked it from his grasp.

"Stop fucking around. That's not a toy."

Miles glared at him and rose. "I've got to take a leak." He disappeared behind the shadow of a boulder.

Del turned to the little ones. "Come on now, soldiers, let's get moving. I've only got three matches left. We need more firewood."

But he couldn't really blame any of them for not wanting to go. Del had no desire to venture back down into that forest either, least of all in the dead of night.

A huge gust of wind suddenly thundered down the mountain like the roar of a landing jet. The fire sputtered and died. A new crescendo of banshee wails erupted from the children.

"Hey, it's okay, just stop that hollering," Del said, moving to heap the last of the kindling on the smoking embers. "Miles, go get the matches." There was no response. "Right *now*, Miles."

He stormed over to the boulder, but Miles was gone. Del hurried to an outcrop above the campsite and looked down the mountain. A backpacked figure was loping steadily across the slope.

"Miles!" Del screamed after him.

Puffing with anger, Del glared down at the flickering lights of Kyle's bonfire. He imagined Kyle and Gillian warm and safe and close together, his hands massaging her legs. They were laughing about Del, mocking him.

Well goddamn you all.

"Light that fire!" Jennifer demanded.

Del trudged back to the others. He cupped his smudged, frozen fingers and struck a match. A sharp gust claimed it before the sulfur even had a chance to burn out.

"Shit, shit," he grumbled. Sweat trickled from his armpits. He crouched beside his tent to escape the wind and struck his second match. It ignited.

"Oh God! Oh God!" Jennifer shrieked suddenly. "*It's coming!*"

Del jolted around, the flame searing his fingers.

She was pointing out into the darkness, beside herself with terror. "There! There it is again!"

Del could see nothing but jutting, white-tufted outcrops. "What? What's wrong? You made me lose a match."

Jennifer stared out at the snowfield with hollow eyes, her look of fixed terror frightening in itself. "It *was* there, I saw it."

"Saw what? You're imagining things, little girl."

Jennifer shook her head, eyes still glued to the snowfield. "It was a man in a big fur coat," she whispered. "He was all red and ugly, and he looked starved." She shuddered. "It was horrible. He looked at me like he wanted to *eat* me." Her voice had the eerie clarity of a child oracle. "He reached out to grab me—but he had no hands! They were all chewed away."

Lissa began bawling hysterically, her voice climbing the decibel scale.

"I want my mommy!" Lonny sobbed.

"Now, Jennifer," Del said with forced calm, "you were just seeing things. Please, everybody, just give me a little peace here. I have to concentrate on relighting this fire." He did not tell them it was the last match. If this one went out, they were dead meat. "Come here everyone, get around me and block the wind."

The little campers gathered in a circle around Del, forming a human windbreak. Clenching the match between wet fingers, he struck it against the side of the box, slow and steady. The soggy matchhead crumbled and fell into the snow.

The kids watched, silent and unknowing. Del just stared at the naked matchstick. Then he buried his face in his hands.

"Del?" Jennifer said. "Del!"

Del plodded to the edge of the promontory, snowflakes swishing in his face.

He had been so sure of everything until now. Of all the campers, *he* was supposed to be the born leader, the one who would come out of this a winner. In any group, he had always been the one voted Most Popular, Most Likely to Succeed, and he'd come to take success for granted. His own failure now left him at a loss. Why was it happening?

Del's stomach churned and growled rebelliously. With no food, no matches, no firewood, he was running out of options. He had a responsibility to see these kids through. Kyle's camp had what he needed, but Kyle hated him. Del could never ask him for anything now.

Far below, the enemy campfire burned brightly through the trees.

30

Gordon

B reathe, breathe, step.

Hunched in a Neanderthal crouch, Gordon shambled along a trail of footprints frozen into the icy slope. A trace of moonglow lit his way.

Ease on down, ease on down the road …

He needed two breaths now to complete every step. The strain of the ordeal was catching up with him. His hands and face were hard and pebbly with frostbite.

"These boots were made for walkin'," he half-sang, half-laughed.

So many blisters had swollen under his feet that he felt as if he were walking on ball bearings. He would stop periodically and lance the blisters with his Swiss Army knife. There was no pain. The abscess on his calf had widened into an ulcerated crevice, the skin black and curled back away from the edges. The flesh inside was spongy and coated with mucus.

Stop now. Sleep.

No, he had to catch up while there was still time. But it was an effort to keep his mind in rational order. He had gone for minutes—or was it hours?—without a solitary thought in his head. Maybe his brain was shutting down to anesthetize itself. Was he dying? Pop Hollos never had a chance to come to terms with death, but Gordon would face it head-on.

He pictured the look on Howard DeRosa's face when they told him how Gordon had perished in the snow like Scott of the Antarctic, starved and naked against the elements. Howard would mourn his fallen comrade with guilt and anguish.

That poor bugger ... no one deserves to sign out like that. It's all my fault, I'm the guy who talked him into going back up there.

"Mush, mush," Gordon called out to imaginary sled dogs, pushing onward.

Howard's face lingered in his mind. *Did you take that red tag, Gordie?* Howard asked him.

"Of course not," Gordon replied aloud, hurt. "It could have been Del—or even Kyle himself. I'm sorry you even think I could have done it, Howard."

But what if he had taken the tag? If he had, it would have been only so that he could rappel down and rescue Kyle. Everyone would have seen that Gordon was a mountain expert, a hero. No mountain would ever mess with him again. There would be no more Cal Wolcroft incidents—not ever.

But Gordon was certain he hadn't done it. He could rest easy.

A bird swooped down low and landed on the ice ahead of him. Gordon lurched forward in a wild dash to catch it, but the bird fluttered lazily away. He hadn't even come close. What had possessed him to think he had a chance in hell to catch it? His moldy teeth clicked greedily. His hunger was driving him mad, consuming his common sense. Earlier he had chewed on bark and pine needles—even gnawed his leather belt into a slimy lump.

Just a little farther. Spaghetti and Spam. Warm tent.

A running brook lay ahead. Gordon slumped to the snow beside a side pool and ripped a clump of sedge from the bank. He slowly chewed the coarse, tasteless grass, smiling at the image of himself masticating like a contented cow.

The brook teemed with tiny fish, silvery in the foggy moonglow. They were barely larger than minnows, but Gordon needed protein. He tried to catch one with his tin cup, awkwardly splashing himself. A half hour of frantic effort yielded nothing but soaked jeans and boots. He shook himself and lay weakly on his side like a tired old bloodhound, watching the fish darting to and fro, beyond his grasp.

Time passed as in a dream. Gordon's gaze was lost in the brook's moonlit reflection, his mind floating in a comforting swirl of fog. Before his eyes, the water gradually turned ice-blue, then warmed to magenta. He found he could change the colors at will.

A fretful thought wafted up through layers of fleecy oblivion: *Am I still snowblind?* The thought flew out of his head and disappeared into the fog, a bird in flight. Gordon painted the fish, the snowfield, the moonswept peaks in iridescent strokes of pulsating color. As if for the first time, he reveled in the stark magnificence of The Wilds. Its scenic expanses far exceeded any human conception of beauty. There was grandeur here, epic and everlasting, animated and rendered even more alive by Gordon's magic palette of colors. Man simply did not fit into this grand scheme, he realized, and felt a sudden humility, ashamed of his own petty suffering.

We mean nothing here, we're insignificant specks.

Gordon could see himself and the others clearly now as worthless creatures, invaders without right or cause. Man had only sullied the cosmic perfection of The Wilds, upset the natural balance. He did not belong here; like Adam in the Garden of Eden, he was a misfit, destined for expulsion.

The Wilds is too pure for us, Gordon realized, touching his seeping calf wound just to register his meaningless pain.

It would be better if all of us perished.

The act of relinquishing his human self to nature's greater purpose felt irresistibly *right* an act of God. As if he had spent a lifetime waiting for this very moment to do something truly good and selfless.

On your feet boy, Andele, andele.

His legs were now solidly caked with ice, the abscess almost devoid of feeling now. Gordon crawled to a boulder and clung to it for support as he dragged himself laboriously to his feet. After a moment he was able to stand free again, stiff-legged and wobbly. He walked, sensing that his legs were deliberately propelling him toward some ill-defined act, close at hand. The act had already been committed on a deeper level, he knew. The future was reaching back in time, guiding him on to finish what was already history.

Ahead in the snow stood a small, forlorn figure. One of the campers? Yes! Gordon broke into a joyful, hobbling run. His legs buckled under him, and he fell. He lifted his face from the snow and stared agog at a boy with familiar blond hair and freckled features.

It was Cal Wolcroft, gazing back with wistful, lambent eyes. The boy was alive and well, his frail body intact. His pale face and hands sparkled with hoarfrost.

Gordon gawked at the flesh-and-blood figure. "Am I dreaming you?" he asked.

"You've got to find the others," Cal told him in a soft, almost tender voice. "Remember what you promised Jerry, remember what he said about Del."

"I know, I know," Gordon murmured. "But I can't move, Cal. Will you help me?"

The boy drew closer, laying a frail hand on his shoulder. At once, Gordon felt a sense of soaring release. Imbued with new strength, he lifted himself to his knees.

"I'm sorry for what happened to you," Gordon burbled. "It was my fault."

"That's okay." The boy smiled genially. "You didn't mean it."

"Thank you, Cal." Tears streamed down Gordon's face.

"*You* didn't mean it, but the others ..." Cal's eyes suddenly clouded and his lower lip jutted out in a pout. "Those new campers, you know, they left you for dead. That was so *mean*. They should have come back for you. That Del should have known better, don't you think, sir?"

Gordon nodded emphatically.

"They were bad," Cal continued. "They should be made to pay the piper."

"Pay the piper," Gordon repeated, dazed.

"Remember what happened to me?"

Gordon nodded. "It was a mountain lion," he said in a cottony voice.

"Think so? It could have been you, Gordon."

"No way, that's crazy. I don't need this."

Cal's voice seemed to be sucking all the oxygen out of the air. Gordon began to hyperventilate.

"What you need is a good meal," Cal said. "Fresh meat. Right now."

"Go away. Leave me alone."

The boy ripped his own shirt open and dug his fingers into his belly until the skin broke with a faint exhalation of fetid air. The hand disappeared with a gurgle and reemerged holding something gray and ropy.

"This is what you need," Cal said.

Gordon retched and struggled to crawl away, his stomach hot and tight. But he couldn't move.

"Just like old times, huh, sonny?" Cal hissed in Pop Hollos's raspy voice.

"Shut up!" Gordon shrieked, flattening his palms against his ears.

"The Donner Man's got big plans for iggerants like you." The ghoul's nose puckered inward, shriveling like a fetid blob of cheese. A serpentine tongue reared out between green, moldy lips, then skittered to the ground. "He's got you now, you party animal," cawed the crumbling creature.

"No … no …" Gordon whimpered, shivering in a putrid arctic squall.

The specter disintegrated into tiny motes of whiteness, a blur of glittery snowflakes that stung Gordon's face.

Rising unsteadily on all fours, Gordon realized that his open eyes had filled up with spindrift. He began to salivate uncontrollably.

What you need is a good meal.

31

Kyle

"Del's losing it," Miles told Kyle and the others as he gnawed on a hunk of stale bread. The campers crowded around him, listening avidly to his every word. "They're out of firewood, they're out of food. I'll bet you tomorrow's rations they'll all be down here by morning."

"I'm not surprised," Gillian said, turning to Kyle. "The little kids expect Del to act like a counselor, and he doesn't have a clue."

"None of us are counselors either," Kyle said. He whittled a hunting spear with his jackknife. "We're *all* just kids."

"Somehow I don't get it," Miles commented, eyeing Gillian curiously. "You used to think Del was cool—until he dumped you."

"Until *I* dumped *him*, you jerk," she corrected. "He's changed, everyone can see that. I don't even know him anymore."

"Maybe you never did," Kyle said. "Look, I don't want to keep defending the guy, but ..." He paused, knowing how it felt to be an outcast. "I can understand the pressure he must be under."

"Look up," Page said. "The stars are out."

A cluster of stars glittered through a gash in the cloud cover, lifting Kyle's spirits. The immensity of the open sky was mightier than The Wilds could ever be.

"That's the Little Dipper," Page remarked. "Ursa minor. There's Polaris, the last star in the handle. Now if we could just see the two pointer stars in the Big Dipper, we'd be sure where north is."

"Gee Professor, you're a whole lot of help there," Frank said. "If we had wings, we could fly out of here too."

It was time to hit the sleeping bags. Kyle elected to serve the first shift, keeping vigil over the signal fire while the others retired. Alone, he whittled his spear to a sharp point with fixed concentration. The work gave him a sense of accomplishment and purpose. He imagined himself the first man on earth, inventing the first weapon.

"Think it'll work?"

Kyle looked up, startled from his fantasy. It was Gillian. She sat down next to him on the log. The ice crystals on her hair glinted in the firefight.

"It better," Kyle replied, "or we'll be chewing on leaves and twigs tomorrow."

Gillian gazed out into the chilly darkness. "What are we going to do?"

"Get rescued, of course." Self-conscious, he shifted away from her closeness. He wished he didn't smell as rank as he did.

"And Del?"

"Who knows? We can't make him join us if he doesn't want to." He blinked. "I guess it really bugs you that he's losing it, right?"

Gillian's jawline tightened. "No more than it bothers you."

"Did you know Del before camp?"

"We'd been going out since last fall. At first, I guess I was mostly turned on by his reputation, you know? Student body president, football captain, all that. My girlfriends thought he was so cool." She paused, tossing her hair back from her face. "Not that he wasn't. Del was sweet. Really open and generous, you know? But for me, it was more *what* he was than *who* he was. All of a sudden I was 'Del's girl,' hanging out with 'Del's friends' doing 'Del's thing.'"

"I really liked Del when I first got to camp. Now I don't know. It's like he's scared, but he won't admit it—he just gets angry."

"He's more scared than any of us because he thinks he's supposed to be the leader. He's petrified now that he's blowing it."

Kyle nodded. "Seems like everything has to be his way or he gets bent out of shape."

"I know. But the thing is—it sounds weird saying this—I'm the same way."

Kyle laughed. "Get real."

"You don't know me that well, Kyle." Gillian set her hiking boots in front of the fire to dry. "Anyway, I don't really care what Del does now. But with those kids, it's a different story. If he's going off the deep end, we have to do something."

"Yeah, like what?"

"I don't know. A rescue raid or something."

Kyle grinned.

"What's the big smile for?"

"Nothing. It's just that you've changed a helluva lot since we left on the hike. You always seemed like Little Miss Perfect."

"Little Miss Perfect? Hah!" Gillian punched him playfully.

"You never used to speak up for yourself. But you're tougher now."

Gillian cocked her head. "You've changed too, you know. You used to be so distant, like you thought you were too cool to hang out with us."

"I hated Wolf Gulch."

"You wouldn't talk to anyone but Del. Then after the accident, I don't know, you sort of came out of yourself. You showed us how to survive."

Kyle felt his face flush. No girl had ever talked to him this way before.

Gillian suddenly furrowed her eyebrows. "Something's been bothering me. I know you don't want to talk about it."

"About what?"

"You know, about your brother dying. What Del said—that you were responsible."

"It wasn't anything." Kyle couldn't stop swallowing; his voice was faint. "Del didn't know what he was talking about."

"Come on, Kyle. You can tell me." Gillian's soft, assured voice lowered his guard. "You said your brother was, what?"

"Autistic." He wanted to confide in Gillian but wasn't sure how much he could tell her. "Know what that means?"

"Retarded, right?"

Kyle deliberated carefully. "No, autistic is different from retarded. Retarded people don't always know what's happening, but with Marshall, it was just the other way around. His brain was so tuned in to sights and sounds and smells that he just couldn't handle all the input. So he cut himself off—that's what some autistic kids do. They sort of withdraw into their own fantasy world, where *they* control what's happening.

"Anyway, Marshall did some pretty strange shit, and that put a lot of pressure on the family. Mom and Dad couldn't handle it. That's why they finally split up."

He pushed the spear into the fire to harden its point. The flames crackled, sending a jet of sparks whooshing over the snow.

"Dad's a workaholic," Kyle continued, "or at least that was his excuse for not dealing with Marshall. Dad just couldn't *stand* being near him. So I ended up having to take care of him every day after school. That's not to say Marshall wasn't a good kid. He did his best, but he needed more help than I could give.

"He liked routines, so I tried to get him on a regular schedule—take a bath at five, help me make dinner at six, that kind of stuff. But I always, *always* had to watch him."

Kyle realized he was clenching his fists.

"The minute I let down my guard, something would happen. He'd try to drink a bottle of Clorox or fly down the laundry chute. Or he'd just wander off, and I'd go bonkers looking for him."

"What a drag," Gillian said and squeezed his hand. "And your dad never helped?"

"Sure, if he happened to be home, which was just about never." Kyle noticed Gillian's hand still resting over his own but was too distracted to react. "The worst part was always being scared something would happen." Kyle's fists began to tremble. "Next to our house there was an old refrigerator in an empty lot. It still had a door, which was really stupid. I mean, people are supposed to take the doors *off* old refrigerators like that—it's illegal!"

"I know," Gillian whispered.

Kyle stopped himself and threw another log on the fire, trying to conceal his agitation. Should he go on, should he tell her everything? "Anyway, I was always sure Marshall would lock himself inside that old fridge. Whenever he disappeared, that was the first place I'd look."

Gillian shivered. "And one time you didn't ..."

"I was running Marshall's bath. The phone rang and some salesman rang the doorbell. By the time I'd dealt with all that, sure enough, Marshall was missing. I raced out to check the refrigerator. The door was closed. It was all old and rusty, and I had to pry it open with a tire iron. I almost tore that door off its hinges."

"So what happened?"

"It was empty. I looked everywhere, but I just couldn't find him. So finally I went back to the house and checked the bathroom." Kyle stopped himself, torn. No, he couldn't expect her to believe Marshall had wanted to die, had wanted him to do it. "He was at the bottom of the tub," Kyle said finally, in a lie. "Drowned in a foot of water."

Gillian clutched his hand tightly. "Oh Kyle."

"I should've been there."

"It wasn't your fault."

"No, I let him down." A tendon in his neck tightened. "I think maybe he *wanted* to die, you know? If I'd—"

"Shhhh," Gillian put her arm around his shoulder.

He fought back tears. "God, I miss him," he said, sobbing.

"It's okay, Kyle. You did everything you could for him, you were great. God, I could never imagine living with something like that."

A pine tree rustled abruptly behind them. They turned, drawing instinctively closer to each other. A brief wind squall rushed through the branches.

"Expecting the Donner Man?" Kyle teased. They both chuckled nervously. Almost in reflex to their sudden closeness, Gillian turned impulsively and quickly kissed Kyle on the lips.

"What did you do that for?" Kyle said, flushing.

Gillian shrugged with an embarrassed smile. Their eyes locked and her smile faded. Kyle returned her kiss, clumsily at first, then full and strong.

Gillian broke away as if taken aback, then turned again to kiss him hungrily, clasping her hands around his neck. Kyle felt her body tremble.

Abruptly, she rose to her feet with an impish smile on her face. "I'll be right back."

Gillian disappeared quickly into her tent and reappeared with her sleeping bag. Neatly and expeditiously, she spread it out on the tarp before the fire. "Come on," she said, climbing into the bag and holding it open for him. "It's cold out."

Kyle hesitated, unsure. Gillian looked at him askance, her hair fluttering in the gusts like gossamer.

"What's wrong?" she asked. "You're not a virgin, are you?"

"Me? No way," Kyle lied with a cavalier smile.

Mustering his courage, he slipped in next to her. She took off his leather cap and pulled the bag over them.

"You're a great kisser," she said, tugging lightly on his ear.

"Yeah? You had a lot of practice?"

"Don't talk."

She kissed him again, her hands reaching for his groin without a trace of inhibition. Aroused, Kyle's body responded fully, but he still felt bottled up with tension, unable to enjoy the moment. He tried to concentrate on Gillian's body, squeezing her nipples until he felt them harden through her grubby sweatshirt.

She gasped. "I want you inside me. Undo my jeans. Quick."

Her pants were tight, and he had to struggle to pull them off. With the ease of experience, Gillian unzipped his fly and guided him into her. She moaned, her voice rising up the scale to a quick crescendo, and she climaxed almost at once. Kyle continued moving awkwardly against her, trying to match her instant passion. But he felt nothing.

"Oh Kyle," she murmured, holding him.

He stopped moving and eased away from her.

Gillian opened her eyes. "What's wrong?"

"Nothing."

Something *fast* suddenly tore into the campsite from the dark of the wood. A fawn. It froze and regarded them with curious velvet-brown eyes, reflecting the fire.

"It's Bambi!" Gillian cried with a laugh.

The animal bounded off toward the stream. The two of them turned back to the fire—and found themselves face to face with Del. Gillian gasped with fright.

"Caught you," Del said. He was filthy and disheveled, a terrible crimped grin on his face.

Hatchet in one hand, he shuffled to the fire and lit a crude pine-sap torch. Kyle zipped up his pants and scrambled out of the sleeping bag.

"What are you doing?" he shouted.

Del grabbed the remaining food pack and slung it over his shoulder.

Awakened by the voices, the others stumbled out of their tents and stood dumbstruck at the sight of Del.

"Look, man," Kyle said, approaching him cautiously, "there's enough food here for everyone."

"Liar!" Del shouted, edging back, his eyes wide.

"You're welcome to share our food," Kyle said.

"Tell him to just leave, Kyle," Gillian countered, stepping fully clothed from the sleeping bag. "He's already taken his share."

Haines nodded. "No shit."

"Yeah, and now he wants all of it," Miles said. "What a fucking pig!"

Kyle silenced them with a commanding look. He turned to Del. "You can take whatever you need, but it's only snack food." Del didn't move. "Go ahead, it's yours."

"Oh *sure*." Del looked wary and confused. "You're just going to let me take it, huh?"

"There'll be plenty of food soon enough."

"We're going to catch a rabbit tomorrow," Page piped in. "They're all over the place. We'll roast it together, okay?"

Kyle took a step forward, but Del shied back again. "It's all right, Del. You can stay here with us. The little kids too."

Del tilted his head, still dubious. "You mean that?"

Kyle nodded, forcing a smile. "We're the Wolf Pack, aren't we? We have to stick together. Especially now."

Del studied him for a long moment. Hesitant but more at ease, he finally lowered his torch.

"First give us back the food pack, Del," Gillian insisted.

"No way." Del tensed again, stepping back.

"Good God," Page said, "we're acting like a bunch of animals here."

"You bring those kids first," Gillian said. "*Then* we'll feed you."

"Cut it out, Gil," Kyle said.

"Stop it, everybody!" Page protested.

"Damnit, it's *our* food!" Gillian cried, rushing for the food pack.

Caught off guard, Del raised his torch reflexively, accidentally setting his own hair on fire.

He screamed and flailed at his burning head, the hatchet swinging. "Get him!" Miles cried, springing at Del in a fury.

"*No!*" Page cried, running in to intervene.

Miles shoved Del hard, hurtling him to the ground. The impact knocked the hatchet from his hand. It flew wild and sliced into Page's chest with a resounding *whish-shunk*.

The little boy gasped in a small cry of surprise, then stared down in wonder at the blood spilling onto the snow. His legs gave out and he slumped to the ground.

Del reared back in horror. He jumped to his feet and fled the campsite with torch and food pack in hand, his hair smoldering.

"I didn't mean it!" he wailed. "*I didn't mean it!*"

32

Del

The crimson penumbra of sunrise found Del crouched in a rude snow trench. He had spent a sleepless night of tortured vigil, huddled over a small fire of pine cones and brush. His forehead and scalp were blackened and burned, his hair crisped away in swaths. His scorched eyes were puffy and oozed discharge. He had been crying most of the night.

Jesus Christ, not Page. Not Page!

He was a murderer. He had committed a sin that could never be undone. The others would never forgive him. Now there would be no comfort, no safe harbor anywhere in the world for him.

Page had been only eleven, yet even at the worst moments he had never lost his head. He should have come out of this better than anyone. And now he was gone.

A golden eagle soared effortlessly overhead toward the Sierra crest. Del visualized himself flying high and free at first, then falling out of the sky like an Icarus on frozen wings, smashing to earth.

It should have been me, not Page.

If only there could be an end to all this suffering, he could become one with The Wilds, find peace and oblivion.

Del sobbed and lay down, resting his face flat on the snow. He closed his eyes, waiting for the sleep that would be his last.

The sun was high when Del awoke; through the thick veil of fog it resembled a hazy moon. He was chilled, but had not frozen to death as he had hoped. And his grief had grown, congealed inside him like a lump of ice.

He relit his pine-sap torch from the fire's embers and stumbled back uphill toward camp. Along the way, Del found a dead woodchuck and stuffed the half-frozen carcass into the stolen food pack. He could not bear to face the little kids; every child's face would be a painful reminder of Page. But there was nowhere else to go.

The children were still in their tents when Del trudged into camp. He paused to eavesdrop as they chattered among themselves.

"I'll bet the Donner Man wears a hockey mask," Marcus was saying. "Like Jason in *Friday the 13th*."

"Don't be silly," Jennifer called out from the next tent. "He wouldn't have to wear a mask. His face is all black and dried up like a prune."

Del stuck his scorched head into the boys' tent. "I'm back."

Marcus and Lonny shrieked in terror and wormed down in their sleeping bags.

"It's just me."

"What happened to you?"

"I'm okay." Del sniffed and wrinkled his nose. "What is that stink?"

He followed the putrid odor to Lonny's sleeping bag and yanked back the cover to reveal a splattering of diarrhea. The boy, pale and feverish, cringed in embarrassment. Del stared at the feces streaking his legs.

"What's wrong, Lonny?" he asked.

"My stomach hurts. I couldn't sleep all night."

Del remembered Gordon's warning. "Did you drink any running water?"

The boy shook his head. "No, only at that creek before the Dragonback. I was thirsty."

"Oh God, Lonny. You've got *giardia*."

"But the water was clear."

Del sighed. "I'll get a towel and we'll clean you up. You could've at least done it in the snow."

"I did it so the Donner Man won't get me. He doesn't eat kids that taste all stinky."

Del felt his belly heave and retreated outside. Jennifer and Lissa were already tearing into the new food pack.

"Hey, easy does it. We've got to ration this stuff."

"Mine!" Jennifer yelled, ripping into a granola bar like a savage bush baby.

Lissa dumped the contents of the pack on the snow. The dead woodchuck fell out. "Eww, gross! What is it?" she asked.

"Breakfast." Del rekindled the signal fire with his torch.

"You eat it," Jennifer said, revolted.

"Hey, I'm sorry, it's all there is. Those snacks aren't going to hold you for very long."

Del slit open the woodchuck's belly and began gutting it with his knife. Aghast, the kids skittered back inside their tents. The animal's hide came away in long tough ribbons. Del had never cleaned an animal before and was surprised at how easy it was. His mind felt fuzzy, as though he were in a dream, watching himself work. He skewered chunks of meat on a stick of green wood and propped it over the fire.

Soon its aroma wafted up from the coals. The kids ventured out again, gathering around him in a greedy circle.

When the meat was ready, Del cooled it in the snow and doled out the chunks. The kids devoured them in silence. No one complained; every last morsel of flesh disappeared into their bellies.

Del noticed that the firewood supply was dwindling, but he did not feel up to asking the kids to play the Firewood Game again. They had already picked the nearby forest clean, and he didn't want them roaming far from camp. It was just too dangerous. Page's death seemed to put everything into perspective now. Del couldn't believe he had taken the risk of sending the little kids out on their own before. How could he have ever brought them up here in the first place?

"I'm still hungry," Marcus said, breaking Del from his thoughts.

"I'm taking you guys back downhill," Del decided at once. "Back to Kyle's camp."

"*Why?*" Lissa whined.

"It's ... for your own good. Lonny's sick."

"But Kyle'll turn us into *Spam*," Marcus protested.

"No, Marcus." Del felt sweat on his brow and mopped it dry on his sleeve. "Miles was pulling your leg."

Lonny stomped his foot. "But we don't *want* to go."

"And you can't make us," Jennifer said with a defiant glare, arms akimbo.

"We want to stay with you," Marcus insisted. "Please?"

Del lowered his head and finally nodded. "If that's what you want."

Buoyed by their faith in him, he built up a blazing bonfire with the last remnants of the firewood. "I'm going to have to leave you here by yourselves while I get more wood," he said, starting downhill. "Make sure you stay close to the fire."

33

Kyle

The snowprints had all the signs of easy prey. Kyle guessed they were from a young mountain lion, a cub, dragging a heavy kill. Spear poised in readiness, Kyle followed them through the silent starry night, deep into the conifer woods. He moved cautiously, but with the swift ease of an Indian tracker. Kyle couldn't go back to camp empty-handed. The others were depending on him. He was the hunter.

The tracks snaked down a ravine into a small canyon. Hastening onward, Kyle picked up a putrid scent. It intensified into a sweet, cloying smell, like a road carcass left to rot in the sun until its innards exploded. A tuft of hair lay on the tracks before him. Human hair, he noted, greatly puzzled.

The stench grew, thickening in the night air; it was unbreathable, almost gelatinous.

Kyle heard violent splashing and forged ahead. The canyon veered and widened into a boggy, brackish lake. A tall man in the shallows was shaking a small boy with neck-snapping force. The man was barely visible in the tenebrous light, but Kyle knew it was Del throttling one of the little kids. He broke into a run along the shoreline.

"Del!" he shouted, waving his arms. *"Stop it!"*

The tall figure looked up. It wasn't Del, but a burly, bearded woodsman dressed in a crude shirt and trousers cut from animal pelts. He had his huge hands around a boy's neck, crushing the life from him. Was it one of the campers? The victim kicked and squirmed feebly.

Kyle brandished the spear. "Let him go, you motherfucker, or I'll cut you down!"

The man grinned malevolently and yanked his victim from the brown water.

The boy was Marshall, Kyle saw with horror. Marshall's gray, naked body flopped limply back in the man's arms like the drowned child of the Frankenstein legend. Kyle began to quiver; he could smell the vinegar sweat of his own fear.

The bearded man scrutinized him for a moment. "Blood brother," he bellowed in the voice of Kyle's father, then bit deeply into Marshall's neck. Blood spurted from a main artery, splattering his buckskins.

"You never loved him," the man cried through bloodied lips. "You just wanted him out of the way. You're the bad seed, son." He swallowed a chunk of flesh torn from Marshall's cheek. "You're such a fucking disappointment."

A hand shook Kyle's shoulder, jostling him awake. "Come on, man, wake up," came the sound of Haines's voice. "It's your watch."

Kyle jolted up with a gasp and looked around in bewilderment at the green walls of his tent. It was an effort to tug himself back to reality.

"Come on, Kyle," Haines said.

"Okay, okay. Just give me a minute." Then he remembered Page. "Is he any better?"

Haines shook his head and ducked outside. Kyle stuck his head out into the daylight; the mountain air cooled his brow. The familiar sight of the fog-enshrouded camp comforted him.

You're the bad seed, son.

No, he couldn't allow himself to believe that, not for a second. If he doubted himself now, the nightmare would return to haunt him, take root in his mind like a cancer.

Kyle left the tent quickly and joined Haines at the campfire. "What time is it?"

"Going on ten," Haines said, tossing a branch onto the fire. "I've got to get some shut-eye." He plodded to his tent, past the bloody hatchet still lying untouched in the snow.

Gillian was awake, boiling snowmelt for a hot compress.

Beside her, Page lay unconscious in his sleeping bag.

"You're going to be okay, Professor," Kyle said.

He unzipped the bag and peeled away the dressing. It was saturated with blood. Page's wound would not stop bleeding. *There's nothing I can do,* Kyle told himself fiercely, not a damned thing. The lips of the gash opened and closed, keeping time to Page's labored breathing. Kyle checked his pulse and could barely detect a heartbeat.

"He needs more water from the creek," Gillian said.

"Right." They picked up their canteens and walked down to the creek. "I just don't get it," Kyle said, breaking the silence. "All Del wanted was food and matches. I would have *given* it to him. It's all so stupid."

"I told you something like this was bound to happen. Del has gone totally wacko."

As they filled their canteens, Gillian glanced uneasily around the woods and leaned close. "He'll be back, you just wait."

"It was an accident," Kyle said in a crushed voice. "It wasn't even his fault. If Miles hadn't jumped him, it would've never happened."

"Del's pissed off because we're all doing better than he is," Gillian countered angrily. "And let's face it, he's jealous of you and me."

"We just should never have left him up there, that's all."

"You're not your brother's keeper, Kyle," Gillian said sharply, her eyes needling him.

Your brother's keeper. The words stung him. Avoiding her look, Kyle marched back to camp in silence.

The campfire crackled undisturbed, but something was wrong. Kyle had to pause a moment before it registered: Page's sleeping bag was empty.

"Holy shit," he breathed, wheeling around wildly. "Page?" he shouted. "*Page!*"

Gillian hastened up from the creek. "What is it?"

"He's gone. Page is gone!"

Someone tall and hulking is dragging Page to a boggy, stinking lake where he can feed in peace.

Kyle plunged into the woods. His leather cap flew off his head in a gust of wind, but he did not look back.

He found Page on his back in a shrouded clearing, arms and legs outstretched as though he were playing the child's game of making an angel in the snow. His eyes were wide open and bulging, his mouth agape, his features twisted in a rigid grimace of terror.

Kyle staggered back, fear overriding his woe. He glanced about the woods, but there was no sign of anyone or any*thing*. No snowprints but his and Page's, no sign of a struggle. Had Page died alone? Had something roused him from his coma, driven him from his sleeping bag out into the snow?

Kyle sank to his knees and wept. The Wilds would not even let Page die in peace. A hungry, murderous power had seized him. It would not be sated until every last one of them had been consumed and absorbed.

They were all going to die.

34

Gordon

Breathe, breathe, breathe, step. Breathe, breathe, breathe, step. Gordon was stepping with hands and knees now. He could still walk if he had to, but it was easier to crawl, sliding wormlike, a few inches at a time. His hands were battered lumps and his knees had swollen to the size of grapefruits. Each movement forward was slow and clumsy, but he had settled into a pace that had taken him through the night and morning without sleep.

Fragments of memories flitted through his mind: tunes from musicals he had seen as a child—*The Pajama Game; Kiss Me, Kate*—and lines from roles he had played in high school theater. He dwelt for hours on the taste of Hawaiian Delight, the last hot meal he had enjoyed at Wolf Gulch. The syrupy cafeteria-style ham and pineapple lingered deliciously on his chapped lips.

Gordon knew his mind was going. All memory of the past few days had blurred together in a crazy-quilt confusion of disconnected scenes. He had only the vaguest sense of where he was or how far he had traveled.

Why drag it on like this? he wondered. *Why resist the inevitable?* There was a reason for all this self-punishment, but what was it? Oh yes … Jerry. Jerry was counting on him. He had to keep his promise. But what promise? *The kids, damnit! The kids.* He mustn't let The Wilds jumble his thoughts or sap his resolve. He mustn't give in to those gray furry clouds congesting his brain.

I'm going to stay alive, I'm going to beat this place.

But at every turn of the trail he feared Cal Wolcroft would be waiting for him.

Build a fire, he told himself groggily. *Your feet are frozen. If you don't, you're going to lose them.*

He halted and groped for his matches, kneeling in the snow. The snow-covered outcrops shimmered and danced before his eyes. The longer he stared at them, the more the snow took on the silken, rippling sheen of an animal's skin, the outcrops rising and falling with the breath of life. The Wilds was a sleeping, breathing dragon, the terrain its bones, muscles, and sinew, with Gordon perched precariously on the scales of its granite back.

The matches were gone. They were not in the side pocket of his parka. Gordon searched frantically. The box was in his breast pocket, but only one match remained. What had happened to the others?

He pulled a few dried boughs from a diseased conifer and ignited a small blaze. His boots came off easily. But his socks were frozen solid to his feet. Stripping one off with exhausted effort, he examined his bare foot. It was a patchwork of blistered, black-and-blue flesh. The toes would not wiggle. He massaged the foot until a trace of feeling returned with a stinging tingle.

So much suffering, and for what? he mused. *For a promise?* Gordon was suddenly struck by the absurd irony of his suffering. Here he was trying to save a bunch of brats who hadn't lifted a finger to save him or Jerry. Not the least of all *Del*, who should have led the others back to the counselors.

Abandoning us—leaving us for dead at the bottom of the Dragonback—that was tantamount to murder.

No doubt Del was pushing the campers onward, never allowing Gordon the chance to catch up. He was probably tucked away in a warm tent just a mile or two away, the tag-stealing little bastard. Jerry had been right. Del was not fit to be a leader; Gordon could see that now. And what goes around comes around, he knew. One day Del would have to pay the piper.

A burning sensation in his feet wrenched him from his thoughts. The damaged flesh was warming, his nerve endings coming back to life and reporting on the damage done. The first tremors of real pain overtook Gordon and quickly swelled into a rolling, tumbling agony. He shrieked and moaned, pummeling the snow with his fists.

Oh Jesus, what have I done? Dear God, just let me die!

A loud thump made Gordon jerk convulsively.

This is it—Cal's come back for me.

An indistinct figure emerged from behind a snowbank. Gordon rubbed his eyes, trying to clear his hazy vision. For a second he was sure it was Wolcroft, then he thought it might be a brown bear. No, it was human. No, not that, either. It moved on four legs. Gordon jammed his sock and boots back on with a yelp of anguish.

The animal shuffled closer. It appeared to be a mangy coyote, its coat ragged and falling out in tufts. The coyote halted at ten feet, bared its foam-flecked fangs, and sank into a crouch.

"Get away," Gordon rasped weakly, heaving a chunk of burning wood at it.

The coyote growled softly and drew nearer, step by step. It looked sick and hungry. It had caught the scent of Gordon's rotting flesh, sensed his weakness, and reverted to instinct.

Gordon heeded the same instinct. "Good boy," he cooed and slipped the blade of his knife into the fire.

The animal lowered its ears and growled, like a roll of distant thunder.

Gordon rolled onto his back in a feigned submissive pose, his hand near the shank of the knife. "Here, guy. Got something for you."

The coyote inched forward, stalking him.

"That's right, Del, keep coming. Good boy." It took Gordon a moment to realize he had said *Del*, but it didn't seem to matter. He would slaughter this animal just as surely as he would punish Del.

The coyote finally lunged with a snarl. Gordon faked right and rolled left. The teeth grazed his hand, but he managed to drive the knife into the coyote's belly. The animal howled and came back at him, straddling him. New pain blazed in Gordon's calf, and he looked down. It was Del, not the coyote, on top of him, his eyes cunning and wild as he dug his teeth into Gordon's calf.

"Get off me, you sonofabitch!"

He struggled, but was powerless under Del's weight. With a roar of fury, Gordon sank his teeth into the boy's wrist and tasted something warm and salty. Del howled and struggled to escape. He flopped over in the snow, his shirt hoisted up, his heaving ribcage exposed.

Gordon stared at the boy, fighting to resist the temptations of the damned. He had to punish Del for failing to meet his responsibilities—not eat him! He tried to think of Howard DeRosa again. How would Howard handle this?

Jesus Christ, I am not *becoming a monster.*

Gordon rose to his knees and staggered onward, following the mass of footprints. Plodding to the top of the next ridge, he looked back.

The coyote was crawling after him, its eyes pink and glazed, its jaws working and drooling.

35

Del

Del dragged a bundle of firewood back toward camp. He hated these claustrophobic woods. Tall conifers hovered over him, scrutinizing his every move; sharp-edged pine cones bristled at him in the wind. He was worried about leaving the little kids alone for so long. He had to get back to them.

A pair of staring eyes caught Del by surprise. A small withered owl was frozen dead in a hollow between two tree branches. He knocked it into the snow with a stick of kindling. The owl was possibly edible, so he lashed it to the woodpile with his belt and headed back to his mountain redoubt.

A frenetic movement far ahead caught Del's eye through the trees. What was it, a wild animal? One of Kyle's group? A rescue team? He tramped through a heavily wooded dell, closing in cautiously until he could clearly see it: a brown bear, ferociously chasing something. Del moved closer. The bear was loping in veering, drunken circles, snarling to itself. White puffs of vapor blasted from its nostrils. The eyes were pink and glazed, the chops foaming.

The animal bared its fangs and lunged around, taking a bite out of its own rump. Bloody bite marks scored its flanks. *The bear's eating himself alive*, Del thought, horrified yet fascinated; *he's completely out of his gourd.*

The bear suddenly spotted Del, who stumbled back, expecting it to pounce. But the beast only glared at him for a moment, panting heavily, and continued its dizzying circles.

Del quickly scuttled back the way he had come. As he passed above Kyle's camp, a brown speck winked at him from the snow. Del was surprised to discover it was Kyle's leather cap. Carefully, he dusted off the snow and tried it on. It was too tight, yet he felt curiously transformed and Kyle-like, as if he were wearing a crown. He missed Kyle and yearned to be reunited with the others. If only it were possible.

Del tugged at a dead limb to add to his load of firewood. The stubborn branch resisted and gave him a struggle. Suddenly, it gave way, smacking him full in the face.

"Fuck, shit, piss!" Del rolled in the snow, furious with himself, clutching his bloody cheek.

A familiar voice rocked his senses: "*Shame* on you, Del."

"Jesus Christ!" Del breathed, staring at the gray figure standing in the snow. It was Mr. Dugan.

"Now, Del, you know perfectly well I don't condone swearing," the camp director said in a severe voice, and hiked up his khaki shorts. His clothes were filthy and ragged.

Del rubbed his eyes in astonishment. "I—I thought you were dead."

"You should not have abandoned us, young man." Mr. Dugan sat down on a rock, and his knees popped. "That was irresponsible. Don't you want to win the Wolf Pack Award?"

"I don't believe this," Del exclaimed, amazed. "Where's Gordon?"

Mr. Dugan's face darkened. "Gordon's very disappointed in you, I'm sorry to say. You're going to have to make up for it. Every camper has an obligation to help his fellow hikers survive. Am I making myself clear, Del?"

Del nodded dumbly. "Sure."

"You've got to take charge here." Mr. Dugan cocked his head, studying Del. "You *are* man enough to do that, aren't you?"

"Well ... sure."

"Good. Then you know what to do."

"Yes. I mean, what do I have to do?"

"You *know* what. You're the food provider, aren't you?"

Del still didn't understand.

"Those children are starving, Del, they need protein. It's your duty as counselor-elect to make sure they get it. You have to do whatever it takes."

"How am I supposed to do that?"

"*Sacrifice*, Del. That's the key. Sacrifice one to serve the needs of the many." Mr. Dugan's eyes glittered. "You get my drift?"

Del reared back in revulsion. "You're crazy!"

"You're a bright boy, Del. Bright as a penny. I know you won't let me down." Mr. Dugan moved closer until their faces were inches apart. "Take the weakest camper, the one that won't survive in the long run. You know which one. Let him serve the many. It's survival of the fittest. Haven't you learned that lesson yet?"

"Oh God," Del whispered, his voice a faint whistle.

"Lonny's the best bet," Mr. Dugan went on with zeal. "He's frail and worthless. If you had the hatchet, you could do it clean and sweet."

"Stop it!" Del cried, cupping his hands over his ears.

"Don't let me down now, Delbert. It's *your* responsibility. The majority must survive."

Del fled back uphill in a blind panic, dragging the firewood behind him. Kyle's cap sailed off his head and disappeared in a snowdrift.

When Del stumbled his way back into camp, the fire had once again died down almost to nothing.

"Firefood!" Jennifer cried, grabbing a handful of boughs from Del's load and tossing it on the smoldering embers. "Come on, quick," she urged the others, "gotta feed the signal fire."

The kids scampered frantically to help her pile the wood high. Hunger and cold had reduced them to a primal, hair-trigger state of urgency. Lonny lay like a corpse on his side near the firepit. His features were tinged with green, and a nauseating odor issued from his body. No one was paying him the least attention.

Exhausted, Del slumped down on a tarp. He had almost dozed off when he noticed the little kids fighting over the frozen owl.

Jennifer lunged for it and feverishly tore away the plumage

with a dull ripping sound. She clawed at the impenetrable ice-hardened belly.

"Let me have some," Marcus begged, jostling for his share.

Ignoring him, Jennifer pounded the stiff bird against a sharp outcrop. "It's frozen," she whined.

"We'll have to put it in the fire," Del mumbled.

"Here, gimme." Marcus snatched the carcass and cut it open with a hunting knife. He peeled away its half-frozen innards. Jennifer snatched a strip of fatty entrail away from him.

"You can't eat that," Del said. "It's raw—it's just guts."

Jennifer chewed noisily, her mouth speckled with blood. "Know what the Donner Man does after he eats someone?" she told the others with a savage grin. "He hangs their bones in a tree."

"How come?" Marcus asked as he tore away a chunk of flesh and wolfed it down without hesitation.

"So they can rattle and make a lot of noise. Whenever the wind blows, it's his dinner bell."

"Stop that!" Del said, half rising. No one even glanced at him. He couldn't bear to watch their little blood feast and turned away.

A puddle of snowmelt caught his eye, and he knelt down for a drink. A ghastly, sunken-eyed reflection stared up at him. His face was cracked and cratered by burn marks, the flesh so emaciated that his brow and cheekbones jutted out. For a moment Del thought the unrecognizable image would burst through the surface and wreak some terrible revenge.

He snatched up a handful of snow and hurled it into the puddle, scattering the reflection into capricious flecks of light. The motes momentarily slowed their dance, then coalesced, reforming the loathsome image. Helpless to destroy it, Del stared down at the Donner Man; their eyes locked. Sobbing, he lay down full-length atop the rippling reflection.

36

Kyle

The campers waited all afternoon for the fog to break, hoping for some sign of a rescue mission. Twice they heard the drone of passing aircraft, but no one came to deliver them from the wilderness.

Something had to be done with Page's body. They finally decided to bury him under the protective boughs of a ponderosa pine. Kyle had chosen the site; it reminded him of his solitary hideaway back at Wolf Gulch. He and Miles dug several feet through the snow, while the others looked on in a stupor. When the body was covered, Kyle planted a crude marker fashioned from the steel shank of Page's backpack.

After observing a bleak moment of silence, the survivors plodded back to camp. Sheets of fog clung stubbornly to the trees.

Gillian broke the silence. "We can't just sit around anymore, Kyle. I mean, what's Del going to do next?"

Kyle kept his eyes fixed on the ground; his mind felt numb.

"He's a menace," Gillian persisted. "We can't wait until he picks us off one by one. We have to *do* something."

"Yeah, like what?" Kyle rubbed his eyes.

"Find his camp, for starters. That shouldn't be hard. We'll take back the kids and the food he stole from us, if any's left."

"What about Del?"

"Fuck Del," Miles said.

"Yeah," Haines agreed. "The hell with him."

Kyle frowned. "What if he won't let us take the kids?"

"Then we'll give him what he gave Page," Gillian said.

Haines and the others murmured their agreement. "That's just great," Kyle said. "You think we should chop him up for bear bait too?"

Gillian glared archly at him. "We'll do whatever it takes."

"My dad's a cop," Frank said, "a law-and-order man. He always says when there's no one to enforce the law, people have to take justice into their own hands."

"What do you think we are, vigilantes?" Kyle asked.

Frank shrugged. "Del's a murderer. There're no cops or courtroom here. There's just us."

"I don't believe you guys," Kyle said in a pained voice. "We're talking about a *person* here. A human being."

"No, Del's a fucking animal," Miles pronounced.

Kyle shook his head. "No, he's only a kid like us, in over his head. He's never had to deal with anything like this. I don't think any of us have."

"Give me a break," Gillian said. "We're all trying to *survive* here."

Sickened, Kyle turned and trudged away into the woods. He snatched an icicle from a branch and clenched it like a dagger.

I'll be damned if I'll have any part of their bullshit. Let them do whatever the hell they want

Kyle wasn't about to force them to do anything. If they didn't want to listen to him, that was just fine. He could survive on his own. He'd never wanted to be anybody's leader in the first place. Yet he couldn't deny the anger and hurt inside. Could it be that he needed the others' support more than he had realized? In his heart, Kyle had to admit he wanted them not only to accept him but to believe in him. Maybe he'd shied away from leading because it somehow meant caving in to Dad's dictates.

But I'm not a kid anymore.

He hiked until he found a mossy cairn of boulders that offered a dry place to sit and think. The fog surrounded him. Clumps of melting snow shifted in the trees, thudding to the ground like Newton's apples. Kyle gazed at the silvery streams of runoff and thought of what Gillian had said: *We're all trying to* survive *here.*

What should they do to survive? Even if they managed to

hunt down a rabbit or two, how much longer could they go on? Should they move on? Or was this it? A bare subsistence in The Wilds that might last days—even weeks?

Kyle started slowly back toward camp, ideas brewing. He knew he must do something; he couldn't count on the others. When the weather cleared, they had to be ready to signal a spotter plane at a moment's notice. He would dig a huge mark in the snow, an arrow just above the timberline that pointed toward camp.

With new purpose, Kyle cut uphill and emerged onto the barren snowfield just above camp. There was enough soft snow here to dig an arrow thirty feet long. Crouching down on all fours, Kyle cut a deep imprint in the snow with his hands and knees, forming the tip of the arrow.

A squirrel scampered by, startling him. *What would I do if Del came charging down at me?* he wondered uneasily. Maybe Gillian was right. Something had to be done about Del. But what? Kyle had been avoiding the question, relying on the dubious hope that Del might come back of his own free will. There was bedlam in Del's camp now, Miles had said. But if anything else happened—if another camper died—the burden would rest upon them all.

37

Gordon

Gordon crawled haltingly across the snowfield, his mouth agape. He forged on through the shadows of late afternoon, oblivious of the cold, aware only of the starving coyote still shadowing him.

All day the rhythm of his breathing had propelled him forward with a force of its own. Sometimes he had the strength to walk, though he moved with the stiff legs of a wind-up toy; other times he could barely crawl. His ribcage didn't hurt anymore and the hunger pangs had faded. His brain had switched off his nerve endings.

He glanced back at the coyote and mumbled, "Go cram it." His tongue tasted foul, a swollen, hairy object in his mouth that made him gag.

Below the timberline he noticed a plume of smoke, then an orange firefly dancing in the shadowy trees. Gordon tilted his head and squinted until the firefly resolved into a flickering campfire. His ruined lips formed a crooked smile.

"See, Jerry? I *told* you we'd make it."

From behind came a shuffling sound. All at once he felt himself yanked to the snow, the air squeezed from his lungs.

Gordon tried to wrest free, but a greater force pushed him on his side. He lifted his head, gasping furiously.

"Del! Stop it, you little bastard!"

The coyote straddled him, digging greedily into his calf wound. Gordon moaned and repeatedly punched the animal's head. But it kept coming at him.

"I'll get you for this, you sonofabitch! You took the red tag!

I'm gonna make you pay the piper!"

The jaws slashed at his abdomen. Gordon felt a wave of heat below his ribcage. He smelled blood. The warmth spread throughout his body, infusing him with a lofty sense of serenity. He started floating into white, fleecy fog. Through clouding eyes he saw Del standing in the snow, hands on his hips, laughing at him. Then the whiteness closed in around him.

38

Kyle

Kyle gripped his spear tightly. He crept along the bank of the creek with silent predator stealth. Gillian, armed with her own spear, followed at his heels. A mountain sheep, young and spindly, was browsing on fir seedlings a hundred feet upriver, unaware of its stalkers. Kyle signaled Gillian to hang back, his heart hammering with anticipation.

The sheep turned its head, catching their scent. It grunted in alarm and leapt an astonishing distance onto a rock ledge.

Kyle hurled his spear. The weapon fell short, bouncing off a tree. Improvising, he seized a rock and pegged it at the animal. The rock bounced off its head with a sharp crack. The sheep grunted and fled clumsily up the side of a ridge.

Gillian let go a victorious whoop and gave chase, quickly overtaking the stunned animal. She plunged her spear deep into its flank. The small animal sagged and quivered, and she pushed it over the ridge. It dropped to the snow with a screeching bleat.

Kyle hurried over to their prize. The sheep's black eyes were wide and all-seeing in death.

"All *right!*" Gillian jumped down beside Kyle, flushed and radiant. Her victory stance reminded Kyle of an Amazon warrior.

"What a team!" Kyle shouted, grabbing Gillian around the waist. The two danced gleefully in a circle.

"I can't believe we really got it!" Drunk with the thrill of first blood, Gillian kissed Kyle hard, probing his mouth with her tongue. He barely had a chance to react when she cupped his buttocks and pushed him back against the sheep. "Come on, Kyle," she whispered. "Let's do it."

"What, here?"

"It's warm." She kissed him harder, deeper, and Kyle responded. He yanked up her sweater and caressed her breasts with matching ardor. Gillian leaned back against the matted wool, her breath quickening, and pressed his hands until they were crushing her nipples.

"C'mon," she coaxed, yanking open her jeans. "Do it."

Kyle quickly doffed his own pants, impervious to the late afternoon cold. Gillian clutched his penis, and he felt a wetness that was not his own. Gillian's hands were covered with sheep's blood.

"What are you doing?" he said.

Grinning, Gillian wiped her hand across her face, then her breasts, smearing herself with blood. "It's warm," she repeated.

Kyle could barely recognize her. He faltered.

"Come *on*, Kyle."

He pulled away from her, all desire waning.

"I thought you wanted to," she said, hurt and puzzled.

"Not anymore." Kyle stared at his blood-streaked genitals. "This is too weird."

Gillian bolted up in frustration and pulled on her pants. "I hate people who don't know what they want."

"Hey, where do you get off?" he said, stung.

Gillian marched away in a huff.

Animals, that's all we are now, Kyle thought, glaring at the sheep carcass. *A pack of wild animals, like Page said.*

39

Jennifer

"Is he dead?" Jennifer asked.

The children peered anxiously at Del's great hulk lying dormant in the puddle of snowmelt. In the fading twilight, Jennifer could no longer make out his bogeyman face. It was less worrisome to imagine him as a sleeping bear.

"I think he just moved," Lonny said, crawling over from his sickbed.

A breeze lifted from the forest below, redolent with the fragrant smell of cooking meat.

Jennifer sniffed hungrily. "Maybe we should go down and check out Kyle's fire." She had found the raw owl meat unsatisfying, and there had not been enough to go around.

"Maybe they're barbecuing a kid," Lonny fretted.

"Kyle's not the Donner Man, silly," Jennifer said with a snort.

Del groaned suddenly, flipping over on his side. The kids skittered back.

"Scaredy-cats, scaredy-cats," Jennifer taunted. She turned at the sound of a dull clattering in the distance. It could have been clay wind chimes.

"Jeez, what's that?" Marcus asked.

Lonny's throat gurgled with fright. "It's the *bones*—Donner Man's shaking his dinner bones in the trees. He's coming to get us!"

"Quick," Marcus cried. "Let's get out of here."

Jennifer nodded. "Grab your packs and sleeping bags. We're going down to Kyle's camp."

"What about Del?" Lissa asked.

"Forget him—let's move it."

The six campers quickly collected their gear and started out, Lonny helped along by Marcus. Jennifer led them down the icy path toward the inky smudge of trees. They traversed a boulder field. The rocks resembled cracked skulls, broken limbs. Goblin shadows leered. Kyle's fire shone out to them like a guiding star.

They were halfway to the treeline when Jennifer caught a whiff of something foul. "What's that smell?"

"Look!" Marcus shouted.

A black lump lay in the snow, moving and groaning softly. Lonny screamed and cringed back against Marcus. Jennifer gathered all her courage and ventured a step closer.

The creature was beyond description, a sickening horror with two heads, one snouted and animal, the other almost human. Part of its body was furry, the rest all frostbite and bruises. The humanoid head rose slowly. A crusted, rugose arm rose in dreadful greeting—or was the creature begging for help?

"No," Lonny moaned, clinging desperately to Marcus. *"No-no-no!"*

"It's him!" Marcus shrieked and scrambled away, dragging Lonny after him. The others bolted off in their wake, tearing downhill in a collective panic.

Jennifer lingered behind, fascination overriding all fear, her eyes riveted on the leprous thing that faced her in the dim moonlight. The beast seemed to pull itself in two. Part of it moved toward her as if it wanted something. Jennifer felt her blood retreating inward to the rapid flutter of her heart. But she stood her ground.

The bloody mouth of the humanoid head opened in a widening O of darkness, letting go a wretched garble of moans and grunts—raving, puling, gibbering sounds that made Jennifer's gorge rise.

The thing suddenly lurched forward, coming at her on all fours. A gnarled hand clawed pathetically for her leg.

Jennifer pulled away easily. "You can't hurt me after all." She marched briskly downhill and never once looked back.

40

Kyle

The patter of running footsteps from the woods alerted Kyle. He bolted up from the fire, where the campers were roasting slabs of mutton.

"Help!" someone squealed. "Please help!" A stream of children barreled into camp at a dead run.

"He's after us," Lonny cried, falling to the snow. "D-D-D-Donner Man!"

"Hey, it's okay," Kyle said, reaching out to grab two campers running past him. "What's with you guys?"

Gillian looked around. "Where's Del?"

"He must be on another rampage," Frank said.

Miles shook his head. "That shit. I'm going to get him this time."

Lonny shivered. "It wasn't Del."

Jennifer, the last of Del's campers, wandered into the clearing at an easy pace, unalarmed.

Kyle turned to her. "Is Del out there?"

Jennifer offered nothing.

Lissa piped in, "He had huge yellow teeth, like a dog."

"Del did?" Kyle said, incredulous.

Lissa shied back, unable to answer.

Marcus glanced around. "Where's Page?"

"He's dead," Miles blurted.

Kyle glared at Miles. "He had an accident, kids."

"Liar!" Lissa screamed. "*He* did it, *he* did it—Donner Man *ate* him!"

Lonny began blubbering hysterically.

Marcus snatched up a branch of firewood and hurled it into the flames. "The signal fire's hungry. Come on, we have to feed it before he gets us too!" He heaved handfuls of twigs and pine needles at the blaze, his eyes widening to a crazed stare.

"Jesus Christ," Kyle murmured.

"I knew Del couldn't handle them." Gillian lay Lonny down by the fire and pushed Marcus away. "Cut it out, Marcus! You're going to scorch our meat. There's barely enough to go around as it is."

"The Donner Man can't hurt anyone," Jennifer said in a calm voice.

Miles took her firmly in hand. "Then take me back to him." Jennifer struggled, but Miles dragged her uphill.

"Don't be stupid, Miles," Kyle warned.

"Fuck you!" Miles forged on.

Lissa marched to the firepit, snatched a slab of mutton, and began gnawing at it hungrily.

"Don't eat that," Kyle said, moving to wrest it from her grip. "It's not even cooked yet."

"Mine! *Mine!*" Lissa screamed, tugging it back with savage fervor. She lunged forward and Kyle felt a flash of pain. There were bloody teeth marks on his wrist.

"Shit." He released the mutton, bewildered. "Are you crazy?"

The children closed in on the meat, fighting over it like wolves in a feeding frenzy. One of them stepped on Lonny, still lying stricken on the ground. Kyle pulled him clear.

"What has Del *done* to them?" Gillian said, chagrined.

Miles and Jennifer returned empty-handed. "Nothing up there but a dead coyote," Miles reported. "Had a hunting knife sticking out of its stomach."

"Must have been Del's work," Gillian said, turning to Kyle. "I *told* you he was dangerous."

"Yeah," said Haines. "We're lucky he didn't get one of the kids."

Kyle shook his head stubbornly. "Maybe the coyote attacked him. Maybe it wasn't Del at all."

"Oh right," Miles said with a snort "Lonny did it, then, I suppose."

Kyle gazed up into the woods toward the timberline. "I wonder where Del went...."

"Who cares," Gillian said. "Let him rot up there." She turned to Kyle. "We can't bother about him anymore. We've been up here for four days now, we've got to do something. The only way we're going to get rescued is to rescue ourselves. If we head uphill, we'll come down the other side eventually and end up in the San Joaquin Valley. There has to be a town there."

Haines raised an eyebrow. "Wouldn't we have to cross the Sierras to do that?"

"Better that than sitting here doing nothing, going crazy."

Kyle shook his head doubtfully. "You're talking fourteen thousand feet. That's suicidal."

"There are passes."

"We should stay put and wait for the rescue people. There's game here, at least. If we go over the top, we *will* end up like the Donners."

"That's your opinion," Gillian countered. "We made it this far. Besides, I'm sick of this place. We're all sick of it, aren't we?" There were nods of assent from the others.

"Well, we're not going anywhere without Del," Kyle declared. "If we leave him, he'll die. I don't want that on my conscience. Do you?"

"Wake up, Kyle. He'd leave *us* to die in a second if it meant surviving." Gillian turned to the rest of them, her eyes blazing. "He took our hatchet, our matches, our food."

"She's right," Miles said. "Let Del get what he deserves. Why should we risk our lives to save a murderer?"

"If we leave him behind, then *we're* the murderers, don't you see?"

"You ought to know, Kyle," Gillian said, giving him a flat glaring look.

Kyle stiffened.

Haines spoke up. "Enough of this shit! Let's put it to a vote."

"Okay by me," Gillian said. "You have a *problem* with that, Kyle?"

Kyle shook his head, his jaw set. "You know, Gillian, you're turning into something worse than Del. A lot worse."

"All right," Gillian said, "everyone who wants to head for the San Joaquin Valley, raise your hand."

Every hand shot up but Haines's and Kyle's.

"I guess that settles it." Gillian looked about, pleased. "We'll break camp at dawn. Kyle, you're free to stay here if you want."

Kyle bristled. "Who said I *wasn't* free?" His words hung in the air, more a challenge than a question. He gathered up his spear and gloves.

"Running out on us?" Frank asked, sneering.

"I'm going out to find Del."

"Dead or alive, right?" Miles said with a chuckle.

Gillian reached into her pack. "Here, you might need this to bring him back." She threw a coil of rope at Kyle's feet.

Kyle ignored it and stalked into the forest.

Del's tents were deserted, a ghost camp. Kyle searched fruitlessly for hours. Where had Del gone? Had he finally flipped out and fled to parts unknown? Puzzled and depressed, Kyle tried not to think about the possibilities and headed back to camp, bringing along the little kids' abandoned tents.

At dawn, the survivors broke camp hurriedly. The young children kept a fearful eye on the surrounding woods, half-expecting Del to come charging into the clearing. His pervading absence worked on everyone's nerves.

Kyle spied the firewood hatchet sticking out of a drift, its shank coated with dried, crystallized blood. He did not touch it. He could not go near it. His stomach went queasy, his thoughts churning up a morbid scenario: Del high at the brink of some precipice, throwing out his hands in despair and leaping into empty space.

As the trekkers moved out, Gillian insisted on taking the lead. But she had to strain to keep ahead of Kyle's dogged pace. They avoided even perfunctory conversation.

As the group bushwhacked toward the highest pinnacles of the Sierra crest, Kyle seriously doubted they would ever make it even close to the top. He kept his reservations to himself.

Despite last night's mutton, the little kids still complained incessantly about their hunger. Lissa and Marcus burst into tears periodically, without explanation. Jennifer babbled to herself about the Donner Man. Lonny had contracted a raging fever during the night and slept fitfully, rousing periodically to vomit or relieve himself. Frank and Miles hauled him on a travois built from two taped-together backpacks. No one mentioned Page.

A clump of snow fell from an overhanging rock, startling Miles.

"What's wrong, macho man?" Kyle queried with a faint smile. "Worried Del might get you?"

"You think I'm scared of him? You're damn right I am," Miles admitted without his usual posturing. "Aren't *you* scared of him?"

"Miles, I've been scared of Del ever since I met him."

"Hey, if you hadn't tackled him when he had that hatchet," Gillian commented to Miles, "the accident wouldn't have ever happened."

"Get off it," Kyle muttered.

The group reached a steep drop-off gorge, probably part of the same one that had earlier blocked their access to Skyline Fireroad.

Gillian pushed back a greasy wisp of hair from her face. "Guess we'll have to follow it uphill until we find a spot to cross over."

"No shit, Sherlock," Kyle said.

Gillian moved on, the others following in silence. There was movement in a thicket ahead. Kyle spied a foraging doe. "Look," he whispered, grabbing his spear. "Breakfast."

Gillian immediately sprang ahead of him, the Amazon huntress on the chase. Kyle rushed to catch up as she let loose a war-whoop and chucked her spear. Before the weapon ever left her hand, the deer spotted them and bounded over a rise, out of sight.

Kyle tossed aside his weapon, dismayed. "You went for it too soon. We could have had it." The two exchanged harsh stares. Gillian said nothing, her face flushed with rancor.

Kyle took the lead this time, and the group moved onward in tight formation. The gorge veered laterally, barely rising uphill in a mild traverse. About a mile up the tree-choked slope, Gillian pointed out a drifted crest of snow bridging the gorge. "We can cross there."

"That thing wouldn't hold a rabbit, much less one of us," Kyle said.

"You think so, huh? Watch this."

Gillian stuffed her snowshoes in her pack and cautiously edged out onto the icy bridge. The snow cracked underfoot. She went to her hands and knees for balance but kept moving at a crawl. Scrambling onto the far side, Gillian turned back and grinned triumphantly. "See?" she shouted. "Okay everybody, come on. One at a time."

Miles moved to go next, but Kyle stopped him. "Let the little kids go first."

One by one the small campers negotiated the crossing, crawling across on all fours, terror on every face. The little kids reached the far side without incident. Lonny crossed with Haines's assistance, though Lonny's queasiness forced the two to make frequent stops. Under their combined weight, the snow cracked in little cap-gun popping sounds. Miles and the others hurried over with no difficulty.

Kyle was halfway across when a rippling vibration raced up his legs, the snow underfoot jittering like a Jell-O mold. He heard someone scream. A jagged aquamarine fracture zipped across the snowbridge like a lightning bolt. Powdered ice jetted up and the crest disintegrated.

Kyle tumbled downhill in a churning avalanche of snow. His arm glanced off a torn-away tree trunk. He tried to swim up through the roiling morass to stay above the surface.

The avalanche came to a bone-jarring halt and collapsed, miring Kyle in its grip. His body flipped backward, one foot trapped in the compacted snow. A flash of pain shot up his leg.

When the clouds of powder cleared, he saw that the avalanche had filled up the chasm with a bowl of packed snow. It was passable now. Miles and Haines climbed gingerly down the avalanche track to help him. Kyle tried to dig out his trapped foot, but the compressed snow contained it like concrete.

"Can't get up," he grunted, frustrated, as the two boys reached him.

"Don't sweat it, we'll dig you out," Haines assured him, using his knife to hack away at the snow. Kyle finally pulled his leg free and tried to stand, but his foot buckled under him. He gasped, the pain blurring his vision.

"You probably just sprained it," Miles said, pulling Kyle's arm around his shoulder. "Glad to see your ugly face again," he added with a grin. "Your little Disneyland ride about scared the shit out of me, blood."

Haines supported Kyle's other arm, and the three climbed out of the chasm.

"We better pitch camp so he can rest," Miles said as they reached the top.

Gillian regarded Kyle clinically, as if he were a bug under a microscope. "Is he okay?"

"He won't be walking any more today," Miles replied.

"I can make it," Kyle insisted against his better judgment, gritting his teeth.

Miles shook his head. "Bullshit. We'll have to make camp here."

"We can't stop now," Gillian protested, tapping her foot impatiently. "We have to keep moving. If Kyle can't walk by himself, then you'll have to help him along."

"Forget it," Miles snapped. "There's no way we can carry him with all this gear."

Gillian stood her ground, her eyes small and stony. "We have to keep moving or we'll never make it out."

"And I say he can't walk on that foot," Miles countered in a heated voice.

"Then he'll just have to take care of himself."

Miles stared at her, incredulous. "What're you saying? We should *leave him behind*?"

Gillian shook her head. "Look, It's not that I *want* to. I But we have to save ourselves, Miles."

"We'll build a sled for him like we did for Lonny," Haines suggested.

"No, Kyle's on his own." Gillian pursed her lips. "That's the way you'd prefer it anyway, right Kyle?"

A long silence followed. Kyle knew he had to say something. "Why don't we vote on it, then. Unless you have a *problem* with that, Gillian."

"You're the one with the problem, not me."

Miles knelt in the snow and unrolled his tent. "Here's my vote, you cold-assed bitch."

Haines joined him. Frank, Jennifer, and the others slowly took off their packs. Gillian stood alone, her gaze averted to the snowy parapets of the Sierra crest.

For the first time, Kyle felt bolstered, not intimidated, by the others' support. He turned to Gillian. "We may not see eye to eye but we have to learn to get along or somebody else could *die*, Gillian. It's that simple."

Gillian refused to look at him. She tossed back her hair and marched alone to the avalanche ridge, staring out obliquely at nothing.

Haines turned to Lonny. "Want me to put up your tent for you, Lon?"

The boy did not stir.

"Hey, wake up." Haines reached out to jostle him, then yanked his hand away. "Holy shit! His skin's like ice."

The older boys rushed over. "Check his pulse," Kyle said. But before any of them could get close enough to examine Lonny, the little kids were already on top of him, fighting for the mutton bone still clenched in his fist.

41

Del

It was almost dusk by the time Del wended his way downhill to the timberline. The snow glowed blue in the encroaching darkness, a Walpurgis shadowland of evil shapes. The weight of his gear had forced him into the staggering crouch of a hunchback.

Ever since he had awakened to a deserted camp, Del had resigned himself to the final, total loss of his leadership. He had never felt more alone, and The Wilds seemed to mock him for his anguish. As he stumbled through the gothic-black forest, he tripped over a fold of granite. Swarms of pine needles scratched maliciously at his face, seeming to laugh silently at his helpless, sickening state.

I know how I look!

Del wanted to blame The Wilds for his woes. It had humiliated him, burned him, frozen him, made the hatchet fly, driven him to irrevocable solitude and shame. But he had brought all of it on himself, he knew that now. What had happened to him in The Wilds? Had he been too sure of his own personal power? Was all this his comeuppance? Did he deserve to die now?

Del had spent the last twenty-four hours without sleep, huddled in his sleeping bag, sheltered in a snow hole he had dug for himself. Windborne snow had sealed the entrance, and Del had let The Wilds have its way with him. He had mused over all the things he would never experience in life if he did not return to civilization: going to college, earning a paycheck, getting married, making babies, growing old. He had imagined himself at eighty, taking his brood of grandchildren out trick-or-treating at Halloween. Finally he had screwed up the courage to set out and find the others. He would ask them to give him one more chance.

When he reached Kyle's campsite, all that remained was a tamped-down circle of snow around the firepit and a pile of refuse. They had left him behind, moved on.

Del scavenged about, raking the warm embers with his hands, searching for a glowing coal. Something cut the palm of his hand and he flinched back. It was an empty Spam can. He wiped his hand on his pants and sucked the salty blood from his wound. Inside the Spam tin were globules of fat. Del licked them greedily, but that only intensified his hunger. He found a charred animal bone in the snow, crushed it between two rocks, and sucked out the marrow.

As the last hint of daylight faded, a puff of smoke in the ashes caught his eye. There was a tiny glowing ember. Del carefully laid a fistful of pine needles and blew until it burst into flame. He fed in larger kindling, then fashioned a hand torch from a branch heavy with tree sap and ignited it from the fire.

Del suddenly spied the bloodstained hatchet stuck in the side of a waist-high snowbank. He drew back from it, nauseous, his vision swimming. For an instant the hatchet seemed to shimmy toward him of its own will. Then came a disquieting murmur of shifting snow from behind the snowbank.

The pine needle fire was burning down quickly, and the cold gripped him again.

I'm going to need more firefood.

Del reached reluctantly for the hatchet, but it was stuck, frozen in the snow. He tugged frantically at it, begging and cursing, until it gave way.

Just as the hatchet broke free, a black crablike hand lunged up from beyond the snowbank and snatched it away from him.

Del flinched back with a strangled cry. A grisly thing in a parka emerged from the other side of the bank, crawling on all fours. Through the layers of peeling, frostbitten skin, Del thought he recognized the face.

"Gordon?" he whispered, still unsure.

The sunken eyes riveted him with a fierce animal stare.

The raw, blood-encrusted lips cracked open and a gibber of incomprehensible mutterings spewed forth.

"Oh my God," Del breathed.

Still clutching the hatchet, Gordon crawled toward the smoldering fire. He forced his garbling into words Del could understand: *"Where … are … they … ?"*

"I don't know, they've moved on. Holy shit, I can't believe it's really you."

The counselor gestured weakly at Del's backpack. "Food?" he rasped.

"No … nothing. We ran out yesterday."

Gordon suddenly collapsed on his side, hyperventilating like an exhausted racehorse. His eyes bulged and he passed out.

"Gordon!"

The man did not stir. His parka and jeans were crusted with dried blood. The wind blew runnels of spindrift across his face.

Del quickly moved to his side, took a tarp from his pack, and set up a crude windbreak with his tent poles. He brushed the snow from Gordon's features.

"Gordon, wake up."

The counselor did not stir. Del touched his lips; they were as dry and rough as Plaster of Paris. He found an ancient tin cup in the pocket of Gordon's parka, filled it with snow and set it to melt on the coals. With the hatchet he cut down a few pine boughs and built up the fire.

"You're going to make it, Gordon," he said, propping the counselor up against the pack.

When the water was warm he pressed the cup to Gordon's lips. Gordon coughed. His eyes fluttered and he drank greedily. Del rose to put a new cup of snow on the fire.

Gordon moaned, grasping for his sleeve.

"Don't worry," Del said gently. "I won't leave you. I'm right here."

Gordon contorted his lips into what might have been a smile.

After his second cup of hot water he seemed to be reviving and mumbled, "Others … all made it?"

Del bit his tongue, trembling, and finally he shook his head. "Not Lewis and Page."

Gordon sat up, his eyes fixed on Del. There was something in his disengaged stare that made Del uneasy. "What happened to them?"

"I'm to blame, Gordon. It was my responsibility." Del held his breath.

Gordon suddenly leaned forward and grabbed the hatchet. He pointed to the brown, frozen stain on its shank. "What's *this*?" he demanded. *"WHAT'S THIS!"*

"It was an accident," Del sobbed. "Page …" He couldn't go on.

"Who did it?"

Del shook his head, cringing. He could say nothing to hide or deny his guilt. It was written all over his face.

Gordon's red, encrusted eyes darkened, ugly and livid. *He knew.* "*You.* You've screwed up for the last time, Mr. Man."

"No," Del wailed. "It was an accident."

Gordon's eyes burned into him, insidiously bright. "You left us to die. *Didn't you!*"

"No, we thought you were dead already." Del felt his own anger building, fire feeding off fire. "That's *not fair*."

"You made us suffer like dogs," Gordon ranted. "Jerry's *dead* because of you."

"You can't say that. It's not my fault!"

"You goddamn iggerant!" Gordon shrieked. "*You took the tag!*"

"What?"

"*You-took-that-fucking-red-tag-and-now-by-Christ-you're-going-to-pay-the-piper!*"

Del backed away, aghast. "The red tag on the Dragonback?" Suddenly outrage overcame his fear. "You're crazy. It was *you*, wasn't it! I left Kyle on the trail, I was coming up the path. I thought I saw you take something—I didn't know what it was."

Gordon stared at him, rooted to the ground, breathing hard.

"It was *you*!" Del repeated in horror.

With an earsplitting screech of fury, Gordon swung the hatchet over his head and came for Del.

"You! You! You!" Del grabbed his torch and fled into the woods.

Gordon bellowed and grunted, his footfalls coming up from behind. Del sprinted ahead, zigzagging through the trees, searching out the thickest part of the forest.

He's coming, he's coming.

This time it was no child's fantasy, no hallucination. The Donner Man was flesh and blood.

Del ran until his lungs burned and the deep snow slowed his gait. He glanced over his shoulder. Gordon had already fallen far behind, out of sight.

He's sick and weak, thank God. He can't keep up. But he will *catch up.*

Del looked around wildly for the campers' trail. He would find them, warn them that Gordon had gone crazy—would kill them all. How could he have survived that fall? By all rights he should be dead.

I wish we were rescued—now!

An idea suddenly struck Del, crystallizing in his mind with perfect, irrefutable logic.

Got to build a fire. A bigger, better fire.

He rushed to a sapling conifer and quickly brushed the snow from its branches. With trembling hands, he put his torch to the bark. The snow-clad bark refused to ignite.

"Come *on*, damn you!"

A clump of pine needles finally flared to life, then flickered sulkily and died.

"Please!" Del begged, trying again.

There was a faint crackle. A sheet of burning bark curled away from the trunk, roaring as the pine sap boiled. A plume of smoke scattered in the breeze. Sheets of flame beat in the wind like flapping sails, consuming the tree. Del watched it, hypnotized by the billowing waves of heat.

Close behind him, a voice whispered: "Do *not* jiggle."

42

Kyle

Torches flickered in the wind-chilled dusk above Lonny's grave. Kyle, Miles, and Haines had dug a hole in the snow on a high pyramid-shaped hill. It was a landmark that would be easy to find when the authorities came back for the body.

"Better make it deep," Lissa warned from a nearby mound. "The Donner Man might dig him up."

She and Marcus paid little heed to the burial. They were too busy reanointing themselves with pine sap to ward off their nemesis, the Donner Man. Lonny's death meant nothing to them.

"Where's Gillian?" Miles said as he and Kyle lowered Lonny's body into the grave.

Kyle shrugged. "She hasn't come out of her tent since we pitched camp."

From the west a flock of birds came winging over the treetops with wild, squawking cries. Kyle cocked his head, staring for a moment into the brilliant sunset. The entire horizon had turned a lucent, phantasmic scarlet that somehow didn't seem right. "I thought the sun already went down," he noted, perplexed.

Something came crashing through the underbrush and dashed by them—a small shaggy animal, moving so fast it was a blur.

Miles dropped the shovel. "Did you see that?" He suddenly sniffed the air. "Hey, I smell smoke."

A burning leaf floated over them in the wind.

"Oh shit," Haines said.

"Let's get everyone above the timberline!" Kyle shouted,

hobbling back toward camp. "Come on, let's move it!"

Thick gray windborne smoke came at them through the trees. By the time they reached camp, great scarves of flame were leaping into the sky.

"Fire!" Haines screamed. "Fire!"

Gillian bolted out of her tent, instantly called to action by the alarm. She helped Kyle round up the little kids as the red dusk grew brighter. Coils of smoke belched skyward, as the fire split into two arms, snaking out to encircle them.

The little kids scrambled for their rucksacks.

"No time for that," Kyle shouted. "Don't take anything—just run."

"I need my pine sap," Lissa cried, turning back. "I can't leave without my pine sap!"

Jennifer snatched Lissa's hand. "I've got her."

The wind blew hot and hard, fanning out the blanket of acrid smoke. Flecks of burning detritus floated skyward in an invisible fountain of heat.

"Okay, let's haul ass!" Kyle yelled.

Everyone rushed uphill, coughing from the smoke. An arc of flame whizzed overhead, dropping fiery debris. Pine cones exploded like shellbursts around them; treetops collapsed on themselves.

"Faster!" Kyle urged, his limp impeding his progress. He spotted a narrow, shrinking breach in the shifting wall of fire. "Through there!" he cried.

Waves of heat roared past them, singeing Kyle's face. The back of Gillian's parka spontaneously burst into flame. Kyle scooped up handfuls of snow and quickly doused it. Surprised, Gillian stared at him, nostrils flaring. But there was no time to say anything.

Kyle moved the campers through the gap in the flames to a small clearing fifty feet below the timberline. A barrier of flame blocked all uphill avenues of escape. Stymied, his leg throbbing, Kyle stared helplessly at the fire. No one could cross those fifty feet and survive.

"If we douse ourselves with snow, we can break through," Gillian blurted.

Out of nowhere, a rapid-fire *thump-thump-thump* overhead drowned out the howl of the fire. A silver firefighting helicopter sailed over the campers from the smoky gloom. It bristled with floodlights and water tanks. Kyle stared up in amazement.

"Dive!" Miles cried as the chopper swooped down in a low pass over the clearing.

Kyle ducked. He heard another kind of roar, then felt the spray from hundreds of gallons of water thundering down on the conflagration. Clouds of jet-black smoke roiled up as he rose. The dousing had knocked a hole in the barricade of fire, leaving a stand of smoking tree skeletons.

"Where's Gillian?" Miles said, peering through the smoke.

"There." Kyle pointed at the distant figure waving at them from above the timberline. "She made it!" For the first time in days his heart lifted with hope. "We're all going to make it."

Jennifer snatched up a handful of twigs and moved to the wet area. She motioned to the little kids. "Come on, we gotta feed the signal fire!"

She hurled in her fuel as tiny tongues of flame burst spontaneously from the smoking rubble. The other children followed suit, racing back and forth to feed the reviving blaze.

"Stop it, you guys," Kyle shouted. "Come on, let's get out of here."

They followed him through the naked, charcoal-black trees toward the timberline. Everything was steaming. A burning branch dropped into a puddle and hissed.

Above the timberline the helicopter slowly powered down, kicking up a flurry of snow. The floodlights were blinding, the rotor deafening. A tall man in a bulky silver firesuit emerged from the craft, his face obscured by the tinted visor of his helmet. He advanced toward Gillian with stiff, robotic movements. The children edged back fearfully.

Behind them, a howling shriek came from inside the fire: "*Help! Help me!*" Everyone wheeled around.

A tall figure materialized out of the smoke, shambling crazily toward them. The rising heat waves distorted his features.

Lissa shrieked and the little kids scattered in a frenzy of terror.

"Hold on, hold on," Kyle shouted, exhilaration coursing through him. "It's *Del!*"

Then a hellish figure emerged behind Del. Was it a man? The two-legged creature ran with the gait of a mountain gorilla and toted a hatchet. Kyle shuddered.

"*Him!*" Marcus screeched, barely able to get the words out. "*Donnnnner!*"

The Donner Man howled and gibbered, coming up on Del in full pursuit. Its frostbitten legs left crimson splatters on the snow. Del hobbled ahead, trying frantically to keep away from the swinging hatchet blade. He tripped and fell. The beast closed in on him.

"Stop! I said *STOP!*" Kyle screamed his voice away. Ignoring the pain in his leg, he grabbed the spear and gave chase.

The Donner Man cornered Del against a pile of boulders. The hatchet quivered and swooped down, Del lurching away just in time.

Blood brother!

Kyle hurtled toward them but lost his footing on a wet branch and sprawled to the ground.

Two hands gripped his shoulders and helped him to his feet. It was Gillian. Kyle put an arm around her neck. New flames were quickly filling the breach made by the helicopter, but together the two scrambled through smoke and falling cinders, back into the fire.

With a fanatical cry, the Donner Man came at Del again, hatchet flailing. But his blows were weak and clumsy, and once again Del managed to avoid the blade. Del was staggering; he wouldn't last much longer.

As Kyle and Gillian neared, the fire at their heels, Kyle caught a clear glimpse of the assailant's face. The eyes were bright and lunatic, glistening like exposed organs.

"*GORDON!*" Kyle screamed.

Gillian faltered. "Oh my God."

Kyle lunged ahead and the madman reared back, brandishing his hatchet over Del's head, about to deliver the final blow.

"Do *NOT* jiggle," Gordon muttered.

Kyle froze. "Gordon, *stop*," he said.

The counselor's eyes met his but seemed to see through him. "We need you, Gordon, we're trapped here."

Gordon's brow furrowed; his face began to quiver.

"Help us," Kyle urged. "You've got to."

A puzzled, almost painful expression of awareness spread across Gordon's face. He finally really *saw* Kyle, and his eyes filled with sorrow. The hatchet wavered above Del's head.

"Please, Gordon, don't," Del begged with a sob, shielding his face with his arms. "I'm sorry! I just did the best I could."

"The best I could," Gordon echoed vaguely. "I just did the best I could," he said again, plaintively this time. "That's all I ever wanted to do."

The hatchet dropped to the snow with a dull thump. Gordon sank to his knees.

Del stood up slowly, momentarily dazed.

Instinctively, Kyle threw his arms around Del, holding him tight. "You okay?"

Still stunned, Del didn't react. Then a great shuddering wave of relief washed over him. "Kyle ..."

Gordon moaned and they turned to face him. The four stood motionless, a tableau of weary, beaten survivors.

Kyle stared at the wreck of Gordon; their eyes locked. He could see the last five days in the counselor's face. Gordon gazed back at him, as if suddenly remembering everything, and Kyle saw his own face in that ravaged countenance. He saw the ordeal of five days that seemed like five years, of obstacles overcome, of tragic loss and sacrifice and triumph. And he knew that no matter how long it would take them all to heal and recover, if they ever could, they *had* survived. And they would never forget. The Wilds, in all its elemental power, had not defeated them.

The cries and shouts of men filtered down from uphill. A helicopter crewman was approaching, signaling for them to evacuate. Overhead, another helicopter thundered in for a landing.

Kyle tried to help Gordon to his feet, but his bad leg wouldn't support him now. Del came to his side, and together they hoisted Gordon to a stand. The hot fire-wind buffeted them.

The Wilds trembled underfoot from the roar of the choppers, its snowfields wildly glowing red in the firelight.

Kyle turned his back to the blaze, and they struggled up through the stand of smoking trees toward the timberline.

About the Author

Julia Teweles was born as Claude Teweles in Milwaukee, Wisconsin. She transitioned from male to female in 2007, although she always identified as female.

Teweles is an accomplished author, former book publisher, film producer, and social justice advocate. She was first published at age fifteen by the National Geographic Society. In college one of her poems won honorable mention in a writing contest sponsored by the Academy of American Poets.

The Stalker was first published by Zebra Books in 1984. Teweles' second novel, *The Wilds*, was released in 1989 by Dell Books and is being republished jointly by Crossroad Press and Fathom Press.

Both novels fall into the category of psychological horror, where the reader is unsure where the evil is coming from. Are the supernatural forces real or coming from the tortured minds of main characters?

Teweles lives in Los Angeles with her daughter.

Curious about other Crossroad Press books?
Stop by our site:
https://www.crossroadpress.com
We offer quality writing
in digital, audio, and print formats.